Death of a Snowmaiden

DEATH OF A SNOWMAIDEN
A Sergey Volkov Mystery

Mathilda Thompson

© 2018 Mathilda Thompson. All rights reserved

Cover Art - Christopher S. Thompson

Set in the last year of the reign of
Tsar Ivan IV
known as "the Terrible."

Only the moon and a few stars lit the snowy path which was quite empty of people, for on any winter's night Muscovites were safely in their homes sitting around their stoves and speaking softly of the day's doings before retiring early to their beds. The meager rushlights and tapers that lit their living quarters extended no reassuring gleam out into darkness. The path, down which the slight figure of a girl staggered from side to side, hugging herself and mewling like a lost kitten, was lit only by a finger of light from the moon. Once she looked up, turning this way and that as if seeking something, then she looked down again. Perhaps against the cold of the night, she pulled up the collar of her jacket and tugged her kerchief forward almost obscuring her features.

Abruptly, a sound intruded into what had been the almost absolute silence of the night, the sound of footsteps other than her own. In fright she quickened her step. The strange footsteps picked up the tempo as well. Then before she could run, she was grasped by the shoulder and spun around. She put up her hands in a pitiful attempt at self-defense but they were easily thrust aside. And any cry she would have made was stifled by the strong hands that fastened themselves around her throat. The struggle was brief and her body would have simply slipped to the earth but for the hands still clasped around her neck. Her slender form was thrown over one shoulder and the dark figure and its light burden continued on down the road, the only sounds the crunching footsteps, the only light the cool thin glare of the uncaring moon.

10

CHAPTER ONE

Volkov ran a finger around the uncomfortably stiff collar of his heavy kaftan. Feeling thoroughly out of place in his borrowed finery, he looked around at the other officials. None of them, certainly not the most powerful boyars among them, seemed discomfited in any way. Yet in their midst he felt like a crow in peacock's feathers. Shaking his head in disgust at his new position in the bureaucratic hierarchy, he thought, "What have I to do with such powerful folk? Better to be a big fish in a small pond than a minnow among all these hungry sturgeon." In spite of his lack of ease, he gave the man next to him a friendly grin. What the neighbor saw instead was Volkov's predatory smile and narrowed eyes with their strangely yellow cast, so decidedly vulpine, that he gave a start and moved away. Continuing to smile, Volkov drew himself up to his full height. "So my appearance can be intimidating even here; I shall have to remember that."

As a result of his restored confidence, Volkov was able to glance around the low-ceilinged reception chamber with greater self-possession. He carefully examined his surroundings, brilliantly frescoed ceiling and pillars, deep-embrasured lead-paned windows which let in only a modicum of meager winter light, and finally the assembled official hierarchs. Between their colorful garments and the lavishly decorated surroundings, the room was ablaze with richness and a corresponding warmth which even the actual chill of the room could not diminish. It was a new experience for Volkov and he was not ashamed of looking around in awe.

As more and more boyars filled the room, he began to recognize certain individuals in the sea of faces: Boris Godunov, a favorite of the Tsar, Nikita Romanovich, the Tsar's brother-in-law, Belsky, a powerful noble, and his own patron and distant relation, Ivan Andreyevich Shuisky. The latter's large and imposing figure dominated the small group surrounding him but when he saw Volkov he detached himself and made his way in a stately parade across the room, exchanging a greeting here and a nod there during his progress.

"Sergey Volkov it is good to see you here," he called out.

"Ivan Andreyevich, God greet you." Volkov found himself enveloped in a bear hug and given the triple kiss acknowledging him as an equal, a mark of singular favor from the powerful lord.

"We have not seen you for a long while, my sons and I."

"The press of business unfortunately, Ivan

Andreyevich."

"What! Surely the cold keeps thieves and other villains near to their own stoves. And the Advent fast must reduce their energies as well."

Volkov laughed. "Ah, but when our good Muscovites are huddled together in one room to keep warm, friction develops and we magistrates are often called in to resolve the turmoil. Though I must admit that a diet of Saint Anthony's fare has somewhat reduced their vigor."

"Still, you must make time to come and visit. In fact, I will set you a date. Saturday next, my friend. I have a special guest you must meet. I've invited others as well and my cooks shall do their best to nourish you all in spite of the limitations imposed on us by the fast. Say you will come."

"Of course I shall."

"About two in the afternoon then. So then, you've been summoned along with the rest of us to greet these Dutch fellows. Mere tradesmen," he sniffed, "surely not worth so much effort."He paused to give the matter more consideration, finally declaring, "Still, they are busy building this port of entry on the White Sea, Archangelsk, and that's to our advantage. Better them, I say, than this arrogant fellow, Bowes, sent by the English queen. How the fellow attempts to put on airs. As if he were of any real consequence. Our turning to the Dutch put a straw up his ass, eh?" Volkov nodded agreement though he was completely in the dark regarding foreign affairs. They are, he thought thankfully, not my concern.

A stir in another part of the chamber interrupted

Shuisky's lecture and word was passed along that the Tsar was coming. The boyars and officials, Volkov among them, immediately took up positions in front of benches set up against the walls creating an almost cathedral like setting with the throne in place of the altar and the rows of officials as attentive and pious worshippers. The Grand Prince and Tsar, Ivan Vassilyevich, entered, preceded as usual by the white clad boyar sons, his personal bodyguard, armed with shining steel axes held aloft. Boris Godunov and Nikita Romanovich hurried to his side to assist him in mounting the throne. "Both favorites but rivals as well," thought Volkov, observing their eager assistance with a shrewd eye. "As to the Tsar, he's been reduced to a bent old man. But still formidable," he reminded himself, "still someone of whom one must be always wary."

Once the Tsar was settled, everyone in the room prostrated themselves some positively cringing, crying out that they were his humble and obedient servants. "And these," thought Volkov with something like disgust, as he bowed low himself, "are the realm's most prominent men." Then sighing deeply, he added, "And I'm scraping the floor with the rest of them." Volkov ventured a peek and caught a look of satisfaction on the Tsar's face at the abasement shown by his nobles and officials. Finally relenting, Ivan indicated those assembled might rise and seat themselves.

Volkov's expression grew rueful. Once he could have avoided the palace, but having caught the attention of the Tsar some months previously by solving the murder of Shuisky's eldest son, he was forced by invitation into attending these tedious functions. Some might consider it a privilege, I do not, he thought. I've no ambitions in that regard. There was another stir and the Dutch envoy and his party were led into the chamber. "How drab these fellows are when compared to our nobility," Volkov told himself. He began to feel a measure of pride in his own appearance and mentally congratulated the Tsar for insisting on the presence of the most important men in the realm in all their finery. "Even," he smiled, "to the extent of loaning garments to the more impecunious in order to impress foreign visitors." He smoothed his own blue brocade robe with more satisfaction then when he'd first donned it in the morning, finally seeing a sensible purpose for wearing it. "Yes, no doubt petty rulers and tradesmen like these fellows are awed into speechlessness." Then Volkov frowned. "But surely more powerful kingdoms realize this is all sham and that beneath this display Rus is a sick land. Military defeats, recent famines and plagues, deserted farms, citizens fleeing the disasters, and," he added softly, "removing themselves from the heavy hand of Ivan." His mouth twisted into a sour smile. "No doubt their spies report as much." He shook his head and caught his neighbor staring at him with a puzzled expression. Prudently, Volkov turned his attention back to the formalities. The formal beginning seemed to be an occasion for an endless recital of the Tsar's titles. At first impressed by the territorial boasting, he quickly became bored with the whole process and his thoughts turned instead to Shuisky's invitation. "Who is this honored guest, I wonder? Who is it that I simply must meet? It would have to be someone new to Moscow surely. Yet I've heard nothing." He shrugged and turned his attention back to the throne.

Now gifts were being presented. He didn't have a clear view, sitting as he was behind a boyar with a tall fur hat. After a time he was hard put not to yawn and gave thanks that at least he didn't have to be present at the interminable banquet that was sure to conclude this reception for the Dutch. At last the Tsar signaled his imminent withdrawal and again there was a general prostration.

After Ivan had left the hall, Volkov saw the Shchelkalov brothers rush to the side of the chief envoy and his associates. "Those are two who enjoy that sort of thing," he thought dismissively, "they've dominated foreign affairs for the last fifteen years and sat through hundreds of these affairs. Well, they are welcome to them," he thought, relieved that at last he was free to go. But first he needed to change his attire and return his borrowed garment to the palace stores. He left the reception chamber along with several dozen other officials who had no place at the banquet.

Leaving the palace and hurrying through lightly falling snow, he located his own men where he'd left them in the area of the stables. Quickly pulling off his rich outer garments, he exchanged them for his own warm, fur-trimmed apparel which one of the men was holding out to him. Tossing the ceremonial kaftan to Luka, he snapped at his man, "Return this. We shall wait for you but don't dally for I'm in dire need of sustenance." He shivered, "It's bone-chilling cold out here." Moving closer to the brazier that was keeping his men warm, Volkov shook himself as when a wolf shakes off the wet and snow, and felt the better for it. "Rus bones like warmth, eh lads?" he said, addressing his men, and they nodded agreement. His stomach suddenly growled for lack of food and he had just began conjuring up visions of hot soup and bread to break his fast, when his chief bailiff appeared out of a flurry of snowflakes. Moving into the shelter and brushing off the snow, Mitka loudly announced his errand at the same time.

"Ah, Sudar, it's good I found you." Volkov braced himself against Mitka's loud tones. Drawing him aside, he admonished Mitka, ordering him to lower his voice.

"Our business is not everyone else's as well."

"It will be everyone's soon enough," replied Mitka in a failed attempt at a whisper, "for it's just that sort of news."

Volkov closed his eyes. When he opened them again, he asked, "A murder?" Mitka nodded. The bailiff was obviously excited about the matter and kept moving restlessly from one foot to the other.

"The whole neighborhood where it happened is aware of it. So word will doubtless spread."

"Who was it?"

"She hasn't been identified yet."

"A woman then. Was anyone seized in connection with the crime?" Mitka shook his head. "Are there any suspects?" The bailiff shrugged.

"It's early yet, Sudar. We've barely begun to investigate."

"Was the woman young or old? What of her class?"

"Oh, young and by her garments and hands perhaps a servant."

"What exactly happened to her?"

"Rape and strangulation."

"A crime of passion no doubt," decided Volkov, waving away any other conclusion with a terse gesture. "Surely you can deal with the matter. You know the procedure. Take a couple more men if you think you need them. I'm returning to headquarters and you can report your results to me there." Volkov noted Mitka's disappointment. Obviously he'd hoped to make more of the incident in order to create a sensation among his fellows.

"Come, come, it should be easy for you to catch the culprit. A loose woman no doubt. After you've identified her, see to the man or men in her life and you'll have a suspect, perhaps one or two more than you need." Turning around he saw Luka. "Ah, I shall be able to return to headquarters. And you can go and solve your crime." He motioned his men to bring forward the horses and mounting quickly, they rode out through one of the Kremlin gates. In spite of the cold and the light snow that continued to fall there were still enough people milling about in the market square in front of the Kremlin to impede their progress.

Mitka repeatedly called out, "Make way. Make way there for the Magistrate. Make way. It's official business, you fucking bastards," he finally shouted in exasperation. The last remark was addressed to several folk who had trouble moving their cart to one side.

"Mitka, the body will still be where you left it, eh? Be a bit more patient with our worthy citizens." Volkov saw Mitka shake his head at the admonition though he continued to plow steadfastly ahead. At least now though, mused Volkov, he's confining his cries to simple requests for right of way. The determined bailiff led the small troop into their own district, the Belgorod. Once there they divided up, Volkov and some of his men returning to the Magistrate's headquarters, Mitka with a small contingent going up another thoroughfare to his own destination.

"Soup, bread, mead," Volkov ordered Luka once they'd arrived, "and whatever else you can find at the kabak to sustain me until evening." He handed his heavy outer coat, hat, and mittens to one of the clerks before retiring into his own office where he stood toasting himself for a few moments near the stove. When he saw one of his clerks hovering in the doorway, he motioned him forward. Sitting down, he began to concentrate on the documents presented to him.

After several hours of work, Volkov was ready to leave for home. "It's dark," he told the clerks, "and time we were all at home in front of our own stoves." But before he could leave Mitka put in an appearance.

"Sudar, I've begun the investigation as you ordered. And the body's been identified. It was a maidservant as I thought." He preened a bit before the magistrate for making the correct inference. "Her owner has claimed the body."

"Then you've no doubt questioned the others in the houschold."

"It was easy enough, Sudar, for it's a very small houschold. There are only two servants, the deceased female and one fellow." He paused to let the information settle.

As usual, Volkov grumbled to himself, I shall

have to pull the information out one small piece at a
time. "The manservant seems a likely suspect. No doubt
you interrogated him?"

"Of course, Sudar, I was thorough. I confronted
each member of the household but this fellow couldn't
have done it." He paused again.

Volkov sighed. "And why not?"

"Why," declared the bailiff with the trace of a
grin, "because he's quite an elderly fellow and isn't
physically up to murdering anyone or for that matter to
getting anything else up either." Volkov shook his head
in exasperation.

"What of the family? Or aren't they physically
capable either?" Mitka nodded.

Volkov laughed and waved him away.
"Tomorrow start with the neighborhood. Ascertain this
maidservant's habits. Where was she allowed to go? Find
out who her friends were. Her owners should have kept a
better eye on her. This sort of thing happens where
masters exercise little control." He sighed. It's been a
long enough day, go home and so shall I."

Stomping off snow and slush from his boots on
his own porch, soon brought servants to the door and he
was immediately divested of heavy outer coat, mittens,
hat and scarves. Prayers in the icon corner completed,
he began warming himself in the comfort of his own
home. Seated in his favorite chair and satisfied as well
as he could be on Advent fare, his wife began to ask him
about his day. "For you promised to tell me about your
visit to the palace." She sat contentedly embroidering as
he described the reception given for the Dutch.

"To me they're mere tradesmen, but obviously useful enough to the state to be worth impressing." He sipped more of his hot spicy mead. "Afterwards I returned to headquarters." His voice dropped off as if something else had suddenly occurred to him and Sofya waited until he was ready to continue. "Sofyushka, do you allow our maidservants to go to market unescorted?" She looked at him startled. "How closely do you supervise the female staff? I certainly hope you keep a tight rein on them."

"Why, Serezhenka, I do all that is proper. Is something wrong? Has anything happened to one of them?" He saw she was about to rise and shook his head.

"There was a body discovered today. A young servant girl. She probably evaded her owners and crept out to meet some fellow. And now we have a murder in our district. Mitka is investigating the matter. But she was the responsibility of her master. They were either careless or she was more clever than they. And see what happened. Still, the culprit should be easy enough for Mitka to find."

"Our servants do not slip out after dark, I assure you," Sofya replied, nettled by the comparison.

"Can you be certain?"

"Of course. Our Matryona, why nothing escapes her eye. We're lucky to have such a good housekeeper." She sniffed. "If you doubt me, you can take the responsibility for the servants yourself. And as for the men, why they are anyway no concern of mine." Volkov nodded, ready to drop a subject that was beginning to put his wife in a bad temper.

"I assure you that—

Volkov put up his hands. "Sofyushka, I believe you. I suppose I am only annoyed because we shall have to clear up something that could easily have been prevented."

"The poor girl."

"She probably brought it on herself. Women of a certain type, my dear, cannot resist temptation. Since they often enough cast out lures, it is no surprise if now and then they catch more than they bargained for."

Sofya shook her head. "It is still wrong to take a life." She put a hand on his sleeve. "You must catch the murderer."

"Of course we will and when we do, he will be punished." He put up his hands to stop any further discussion. "Ah, I'm sorry I brought up the whole sordid subject. I should know better than to bring news of such things into our peaceful home. I have enough of theft, mayhem, and worse at headquarters. One needs a haven of quiet without a sullied atmosphere." He nodded towards the stove largely occupying one corner of the room. "And our stove, she gives us such satisfying warmth A maiden stands in the house and her braid is outside."

"How clever a riddle Serezhenka, that is the stove of course and the smoke that comes from her."

"But here all warmth does not come only from the stove." Volkov smiled at his wife and she gave him an answering smile. And so the Volkov household was once again restored to its usual tranquil state.

CHAPTER TWO

On Saturday, after a brief visit to the Kremlin to arrange for the transfer of certain cases in the which higher officials would have the final say, Volkov and the escort he needed to serve his consequence, rode towards the Shuisky residence. With the first genuine smile he'd been able to produce in several days, he observed the activity on the frozen river. He pulled up his mount in order to get a better look. Numerous skaters, some adept, others clumsy and faltering, were navigating the Moskva. There were sleighs on the ice as well causing the skaters to scurry frequently to the safety of the river banks. His own breath and the breath of his horse hung frostily in the air. With a mittened hand he absentmindedly patted the horse's neck. "Cold it is, yet on a clear day, even winter has its charms," he whispered. "And better the frozen ground then the mires of spring and autumn." He urged his mount forward

24

again, then laughed aloud and shook his head at one
fishmonger's offer of a fish from his stock which he was
brandishing by its solidly frozen tail. The folk he passed
were for the most part somber and so well bundled up
against the cold as to make them appear as round as
blinis.

Volkov missed the cries of the pie and roasted
chestnut vendors. "Ah, well, they will return for the
Christmas season." Meanwhile he felt a perpetual hunger
because of the strict fast imposed on the Orthodox and
wondered what Shuisky's cooks could possibly hope to
achieve in the way of sustenance. "My own energy level
is down," he grumbled. "The church really ought to
exempt magistrates and their men." He looked at the
back of his sturdy bailiff who was riding in front. "I
daresay even Mitka is a few pounds lighter though his
favorite food isn't prohibited." He couldn't imagine
Mitka without the reek of garlic and laughed a bit at the
thought. "I daresay we're all a bit thinner but it's hard to
tell under all these layers of winter attire." Mitka turned
in the saddle and caught Volkov chuckling. He smiled
himself because his master seemed in a better frame of
mind.

Their small party reached the Shuisky estate
which was spread out on a large plot of land like a
country manor and protected by a high wooden fence
even though it was within the walled precincts of one of
the city's several districts. The huge double gates were
open and other horsemen and their escorts were
competing for entry. After Volkov rode in, his men went
off with members of the Shuisky staff, and he and
several other guests were led up broad stairs swept free

of the snow and into a long and spacious hall. Ivan Andreyevich stood ready to greet them all with a hearty embrace.

"Welcome to my home, yes, my dear Sergey Volkov, ah, Bogdan Petrovich, and my friend, Roman Semyonovich. Welcome and be seated. Soon I shall offer you my bread and salt." As the big man turned to greet newcomers, servants stepped forward to take coats, hats, and mittens. Volkov and the others then turned towards the icons, bowed, and recited a few brief prayers. Volkov nodded to those he knew, then sat down relaxing in the warm and cozy room and began to converse of this and that, all the while observing his kinsman still acting the genial host, a role he could play to perfection.

"Pour for my friends, for it is not promises that fill a cup but the pouring," ordered Ivan Andreyevich in a loud carrying voice and servitors rushed forward with cups and ewers of mead. "Food will follow shortly, my friends, but first a drink of this honey mead, eh?" Soon the table was covered with flagons and flasks, chased silver goblets, and even a gilded cup or two. Volkov looked over his own cup at the others present. He saw Shuisky's two sons, in conversation with a few of the younger men present.

Turning to the older men, Volkov recognized most of them and wondered again who it was that they had all been invited to meet. He saw no one unusual. Pyotr Mikhailovich, a young dandy and close friend of Shuisky's deceased eldest son, nodded to him and after a moment, approached.

"So, Magistrate, who is this special fellow we have all been summoned to meet?"

"I have been wondering about him myself but have no more notion than you, Pyotr Mikhailovich. How goes it with you?"

"Well enough." The young man paused, put on a serious look and sat down next to Volkov. He drank from his cup and Volkov fancied that he had more to say, a confidence to reveal perhaps. As Pyotr Mikhailovich drank from his two-handled cup, he turned it round and round as if admiring the craftsmanship the silversmith had put into it. Finally he looked up. "I've become a serious fellow, Magistrate, I am studying politics. The court has become my new hunting field."

"It's safer going after wild boar," snorted Volkov.

"No, no, though it's true one has to learn all sorts of new tricks. Still, it is at least as exciting as a good hunt." He laughed when he saw Volkov's continued dubious expression.

Volkov returned his smile. "No that is not a pastime for me. However, I wish you all the best in your new pursuit and hope, Pyotr Mikhailovich, that you will take no spills." At that point Shuisky stopped the flow of conversation by calling everyone to attention.

"Silence for a moment, kinsmen, friends. I know that your curiosity has been aroused about our special guest. Well, I have gathered you here today to meet a very extraordinary man." His voice rose stilling the last few whispers, the last shuffling of feet, the last clink of cups. "Indeed, a saint has come among us. His reputation for healing and preaching came to my ears long before he set foot here in Moscow. The Metropolitan has already welcomed Otyets Yakov and now I am equally pleased and blessed to have this good man in my home.

So take your seats around the table and I shall introduce him to you. He and our chaplain are with the women at the moment." Shuisky's expression clouded briefly. "After the death of our son, my good woman was greatly distressed. Indeed, she has not been the same since that terrible time. But this holy man had only to lay his hands upon her and, ah, the change that came over her. Her spirit was soothed."

Volkov sat back in surprise. It was true that ascetics, holy fools, wandering preachers, and the like were highly regarded by folk of every class. Even the Grand Prince usually treated such folk with respect as well as caution but Volkov had never thought of Shuisky as a man who dwelt on matters spiritual with any real interest. Perhaps the death of his son caused the change. Now that he thought about it, Volkov recalled hearing rumors about a powerful preacher and wandering holy man who'd come to Moscow from somewhere in the east. He and Pyotr Mikhailovich exchanged glances. His interest was aroused and he could see that the young man was equally curious. Yet his own curiosity was tempered by a certain distaste. He remembered one such fellow from his youth and it was not a good memory.

Shuisky went to the woman's quarters and returned with three men. The family chaplain, Volkov recognized. Of the two remaining men, one was relatively nondescript, short, stout, colorless and forgettable. Volkov concentrated his attention on the last man. Tall, gaunt, dark, intense, his hands were piously folded across his chest. At first sight, Volkov dismissed the man, for his rusty black garments, dark oily hair, and scraggly beard, seemed plebeian and singularly

unattractive. Then he remonstrated with himself,
"Surely, a holy man needn't be handsome, or even clean
for that matter. I should overlook the man's appearance,
forget the past, and at least listen to the fellow." He
continued examining the man as he was sure others were
doing as well. Shuisky's praises fell mostly on deaf ears
for they were all intently staring at the starets. Some
stroked their beards thoughtfully, others covered their
ample bellies with their hands as if protecting them from
his gaunt recrimination. The man stood quietly returning
their stares, his hands now posed in an attitude of prayer.

"Bless our food, Otyets," urged Shuisky. "Then
perhaps after we've eaten a bit, you will speak to us."
The man nodded, bowed his head and began to pray. His
voice was rich and deep, surprisingly full-bodied for so
spare a man. After the blessing, the guests settled
themselves and began to eat. Volkov was close enough
to the head of the table to see the starets very well. He
had to admit he was interested but felt himself both
drawn and repelled at the same time.

Pyotr Mikhailovich leaned closer and whispered,
"What do you make of him?"

Volkov shook his head. "I don't know yet." He
repels me, he thought, noting the man's dirty nails and
stained kaftan. His lank hair was greasy. Yet, he berated
himself, if he denies himself the amenities and lives
simply, surely this is to be admired. They were eating
mushroom broth full of root vegetables and the table was
heaped with bread and pickled condiments. The guests
were dipping the bread in their soup. Shuisky's cooks
had out done themselves in spite of the Advent
restrictions against dairy products, for there were also

turnip puddings, pies filled with millet and peas, and it
being Saturday there was caviar, fresh and pressed,
caviar patties, and caviar simmered in vinegar and poppy
juice, and fish of all kinds, cooked in a multitude of
ways. And the starets ate of it all with gusto.

"Paugh, this is no ascetic," thought Volkov. "This
one likes his food well enough." He noted that the fellow
seemed to be eating more than Ivan Andreyevich, a
noted trencherman. Volkov looked with distaste at the
gleaming droplets of broth on the man's beard. He was
amazed that with such an appetite the man remained as
spare as he was. Continuing to scrutinize him, he
suddenly found his gaze returned. To his annoyance the
unrelenting and powerful scrutiny of the man caused
Volkov to drop his eyes first and he murmured
imprecations under his breath in annoyance.

Looking down at his food, Volkov's thoughts
turned back to the past. When he'd been about thirteen,
his parents had welcomed just such a man into their
home. Young Volkov couldn't like the man and resented
the food and attention lavished on him. When he'd
shown his dislike too openly, he'd been severely
reprimanded. Even after all these years the memory of
that reproof still stung. He recalled how the affair had
ended. He'd come upon the 'holy man' humping one of
the maidservants in the stable and remembered with
loathing the man's fat, hairy buttocks grinding up and
down on a girl for whom he'd harbored a secret desire
himself. He could still hear the moaning and groaning
the bastard had produced in his ecstasy. Volkov had run
and gotten his father and the 'holy man' had been booted
out within the hour followed by a stream of his father's

curses. He smiled with satisfaction at the recollection of how the fellow had been forced to scurry away. He could still see him stopping frequently to retrieve possessions that kept slipping into the dust of the road. And each time the fellow paused, he cast a fearful look over his shoulder, for Volkov's father in a temper was a fiercesome man.

"He has a strong eye, that one," whispered Pyotr Mikhailovich. Volkov silently agreed. Now the man was rubbing his hands together; they were long-fingered and not at all coarse for someone who otherwise looked like a peasant.

"No, no I cannot like this fellow," thought Volkov. "I can't seem to help myself," he added, dissatisfied with his instant bias. He saw Ivan Andryevich press food upon the man and he continued to devour everything placed before him. He drank readily as well. Volkov's glance happened to fall on the chaplain and he noted a look of resentment quickly suppressed. Then he glanced towards the man attending the starets, "That nondescript fellow, avidly following every move the starets makes as if every belch were sacred, is surely one of his disciples. Ah, Sergey, curb your dislike," Volkov told himself, "give the fellow a chance to prove his worth when he speaks. Surely some of these men are truly holy ones."

The servants continued to pour and the guests to eat and drink until Shuisky suddenly banged his fist on the table making the cups and platters rattle. "Now, my friends, let us hear what Father Yakov has to say before we're all so drunk his words won't do us any good." He laughed loudly and his guests joined him but when the

starets rose there was sudden respectful silence. He
looked them over for what seemed a considerable length
of time before he actually began to preach.

"Brothers in Christ, " he finally began, "I am only
a poor unlearned sinner. If I have any gifts to persuade
you to a life filled with less sin and more goodness and if
I am able to heal folk from divers ailments, it is only
because God has seen fit to allow it." The starets cast
down his eyes. In a simulation of humility, thought
Volkov, skeptically. When the starets looked up again it
seemed as if his eyes focused directly on Volkov. Others
turned to see where the glance has fallen and Volkov felt
decidedly uncomfortable, briefly wondering if the man
could possibly read his thoughts. Then to his relief the
eyes of the starets left him and instead turned upward;
his expression grew rapt. "Listen sons of man. Listen
rich and poor," he said insistently, his voice growing
both in volume and in fervor. "Blessed are those that fear
God and follow the truth of His ways." The man's eyes
closed for a moment turning inward to something only
he could see but which was not visible to any of the rest
of them. Then he opened them again and recaptured their
attention with another of his penetrating glances.

"I, a great and unlearned sinner, shall now create
words so that You might be glorified." The starets began
to relate stories of holy saints, giving them as examples
of the ideal for which all men must strive declaring that
these were the suns that gave warmth to the Russian
land. And the company heard again the old tales of Boris
and Gleb, those princely martyrs, so representative
among the Rus of the sanctity achieved through
meekness and suffering.

Volkov was surprised by the text of Father Yakov's sermon. He'd expected the usual fire and brimstone. Instead the man's words were soothing and if Volkov sometimes lost the meaning of what was said, the general context and the rich, sonorous voice, by no means loud, but invasive nonetheless, gave him a sense of peace. "Truly, this man does have a power," he said to himself as he listened to the story of suffering and death that purified and redeemed. The starets continued by describing the humble and pious life of Theodosius of Kiev and how he should be an example for them all. He ended his sermon simply, by saying, "His mercy was revealed and He delivered His people and showed mercy to His servants." The company was moved enough so that total silence greeted these last words until Shuisky broke into the quiet.

"Give us another blessing, Otyets." A sign of the cross was made over the guests and the words of blessing spoken. Then the starets leaned towards his host and spoke a few words. "Yes, yes," announced Ivan Andreyevich, "the good father is going to leave us now and return to the monastery where he is presently residing." At Shuisky's signal a servant hurried forward, a rusty black cloak in his hand. Before he could assist the man, the disciple seized the garment permitting no one else to touch his master.

After they left, the guests went back to their drinking but the atmosphere was quieter than before, not the usual boisterous camaraderie of upper class repasts in Moscow. There was a general consensus that they'd met an impressive man and were relieved that he didn't preach the usual hellfire sermon.

"A man of sincerity, Magistrate, don't you agree?" offered Pyotr Mikhailovich. "He surely inspires one."

"Are you then ready to cast off the world and live for Christ?" Volkov asked slyly.

The young dandy was taken aback by the question. "Why, of course, one, ah, must give these things considerable thought," he finally stammered. "But at least the fellow makes one think, don't you agree?"

Volkov did indeed agree and sank back into a private conversation with himself. "I still don't like him. He's a contradiction. A man who preaches suffering and self-denial and savors his food. A man with the eyes of an ascetic, yet there is something sensual about him, one can see it in his hands, in his mouth, in that fleshy nose of his and even in his voice. He irks me. Is it just because he stared me down, not a thing that many men can do? He's like our Prince that way. But one cannot stare down one's tsar and this man, as he says, is only a humble fellow. I sense an arrogance there. Yet his sermon was moving. Indeed he moved us all." He looked thoughtfully at the other guests, still subdued, still caught up in the fervor of Father Yakov's words. Then someone spoke to Volkov and he left off musing and conversed of other things until the company broke up and with their escorts and lanterns to light the way, rode out into the winter night.

34

CHAPTER THREE

On Monday the week's routine began again. Volkov was kept busy dictating first to one clerk then to another, hearing petitions, and issuing directives. Still later, dissatisfaction evident in his features, he sat listening to one of his clerks read the latest gust of edicts from the Kremlin. A knock at the door made him motion for silence. "Come in," he called out. Mitka strode into the room. He nodded towards the clerk and Volkov ordered the man from the room, Mitka shutting the door behind him. The bailiff, Volkov noted, was so perturbed that he seemed for once indifferent to letting his small world in on the latest news.

"What's amiss?"

"Ah, Sudar, still another murder in our district. Another young woman, rather a very young girl, a child almost." Mitka paused to mumble brief prayers for the deceased his face taking on a lugubrious expression until

Volkov ordered him to continue. "It was another strangulation. Rape as well I think. And," he leaned closer and dropped his voice to less than its usual roar, "it is as if it were done by the same person as the other. There are many similarities. Yet they were at opposite ends of our district." He shook his head in puzzlement. "Sudar, how do I proceed?"

"What are the similarities?"

"Well, of course, the way she was strangled. Manually, for one can see the imprint of the fingers. And the possible rape as well. But also both victims were left by wayside shrines, propped up against them. And surely they were moved there because otherwise no signs of struggle were evident. It is as if they were carried there. Perhaps so they couldn't be traced back to a site which might identify the murderer."

"We shall go to the site of the latest murder and I shall see for myself. Have my horse saddled and add Luka to our complement of men." Looking relieved, Mitka left to gather up the escort while Volkov informed his clerks he was leaving on urgent business. As he strode purposefully from the room, they looked after him obviously disappointed by the lack of information and began whispering among themselves.

The small company of men rode to a more remote part of their district to a street where the homes were flush with the road on one side. Opposite was pasture for grazing, or at least so it seemed, for it was appeared to be a flat field with only snow-covered undulations, no houses or trees, and only a very few shrubs.

"See, Gosudar, it is as I said." Mitka pointed

towards a small roofed wayside shrine and the object underneath. "I left two guards here to make folk keep their distance." Volkov dismounted and, striding past the curious onlookers and the guards, moved in for a closer view. He shuddered when he saw the body; nonetheless he bent over the victim, frozen and only partly concealed by white drifts of snow. Someone had brushed away a bit of the snow but it was accumulating again. Volkov motioned Mitka closer.

"As you said, a woman, a girl rather, and strangled by the looks of it." She might have been pretty for all Volkov knew, but with her eyes bulging and a swollen tongue thrust out between her teeth she looked anything but attractive. Grotesque would be a better description, thought Volkov. He grew sad for a moment, thinking of his own small daughter. "It is wrong when a young life is snuffed out before it has a chance to burn brightly," he murmured. Louder, he ordered, "Brush the rest of the snow away, let us see all of the victim." He grew angry when he saw that she'd been pulled up and placed against the wayside shrine like an offering. An obscene offering as well since her skirts were raised and her nakedness exposed. He stooped to get a better view of the victim's throat. "Strangled by hand as you said." He stood up, snarling impatiently at Mitka, "Get something to throw over the body. She needn't be an object of curiosity for the whole fucking neighborhood." He looked out across the crowd of men and women. "Do any of these know her?"

Mitka queried the guards, "Has anyone come forward?" They shook their heads.

Arms akimbo, Volkov faced the crowd. "Unless

someone here is related to the victim or knows her or has anything to say about this murder return at once to your homes." He nodded to Mitka. The bailiff and the guards began to push the people back and except for three men, they slowly returned to their homes or work-places still looking over their shoulders, whispering among themselves and shaking their heads. "Who are these fellows?" he demanded of Mitka, pointing to the three men who remained.

"They found the girl." Volkov put his mittened hands under his armpits. In spite of his fur hat, heavy coat, and lined boots, standing about was making him cold.

"Since no one has come forward and claimed her, borrow a cart and have two of our men take the body to the house of the dead. I shall examine the victim there. It's too cold here. And Mitka, send someone to fetch your wife. Have him take her to view the body. I want to know if she's been raped. Your woman's willing to do this, eh? She's prepared bodies for burial."

"Of course, Sudar, I will send Luka."

Volkov looked around. The snow flurries had ceased. A weak winter sun was making one last attempt to warm the scene before it set. He looked at the three men standing huddled together a short distance away. "Do these fellows live hereabouts?"

"Just across the way," said Mitka, pointing to a small house on the other side of the road.

"Then let's go there and question them, in out of this fucking cold."

"Gosudar, you are welcome in my home," piped up the oldest of three. He led the way, Volkov, Mitka, and the others following.

"Send all but two of our men home, Mitka. We can't all fit into this fellow's few rooms. Besides, two guards are all we need." He entered a small side yard; it looked neat enough covered as it was by an earlier snowfall, as yet relatively untouched and pristine and pure in its whiteness. The men went up a few stairs into the large room that served the family both for sleeping and eating. Mitka stationed the two remaining guards to stand just inside the door. Volkov noticed the eldest of the three men eyeing him warily. He took in the shelf of icons near the stove and the women timidly clustered beneath them. Bowing towards the icons, he said a brief prayer for the victim. Volkov's piety seemed to reassure the family. When he sat down on a stool Mitka pushed forward, they heaved something like a collective sigh of relief. The old man with his full patriarchal beard was to all appearances the head of the family. As he called out to one of the women, she stepped forward offering the traditional bread and salt.

"We are humble, my Lord, but we know how to welcome someone to our home." Volkov nodded.

"Tell my Lord what you know," ordered Mitka.

"These are my sons," began the old man, launching into his tale and pointing to the two burly men who'd huddled together with him in the street. "We left early this morning for work and noticed that a large object lay hidden by snow under Our Lord's shrine. That is a level area. We thought, ah, perhaps, some poor drunken soul fell there during the night and froze to death for the shape looked suspiciously like a body. It happens far too often." Volkov nodded agreement and gestured for the man to continue. "One of my sons began to brush away the snow from the object. When we saw what it was, why we were greatly frightened. I sent my Vanka for your bailiff at once. We touched nothing further, believe me, my Lord. It is a great evil that has been done." He quickly crossed himself to avert any possible danger to himself.

Volkov turned to Mitka. "When exactly did the snow begin to fall?"

"Around one in the morning. I've already inquired about that."

"So the victim was placed there sometime in the night."

Mitka nodded agreement, adding, "I saw it was dry under the body when the men just now turned it over; so it must have been put there before one o'clock." Volkov turned his disconcerting lupine eyes on the old man and his sons. "Did you see anything suspicious last night? Or hear anything? You are after all almost directly across the road from the shrine."

"No, we heard nothing, my Lord. We have already discussed this among ourselves and asked the women as well. Indeed, there are shrubs in our yard, covered with snow now, that partially obscure the road. We took care of our evening chores, then went to bed. For what is there to stay up for so late at night when we must be up early for our work? We are carters, you see. And proud of it too, Gosudar, better anytime than to be ploughman."

Volkov looked at them all carefully in turn. He had an instinct for these things and believed the man was being truthful. Nor had any of the man's immediate neighbors recognized the victim so she must be a stranger to this particular area. In any case the family could all vouch for one another, since it was obvious they all slept in the same room. He noted the bedding for the elders atop the stove and the rolled up felt mattresses that would cover the extended benches in the evening for the sons and their wives and children. Through an open door into the next room, Volkov could see more of the same and that the second room was used for storage as well. He scrutinized the women. They were obviously timid in the face of the authority that he represented, yet didn't act guilty in any way.

"I repeat, did any of you know who that was out there?"

"No, my Lord," insisted the old man.

Addressing his superior, Mitka offered, "It is as I said she could have been murdered elsewhere and disposed of here. And the only footprints seem to have been made by these fellows here."

"The murderer's were probably covered by the same snowfall that covered the body. What is important now, is to identify the victim." Volkov said this as he rose to go. While the warmth of the room was welcome, the almost overwhelming smells of close confinement, the rancid tallow from the cheap candles, the sweat, the odor of cooking, even the smell of wet fur and sheepskin, were not. "I want some sort of barrier set around the scene; then brush away the snow carefully, there may be something underneath. You shall direct that operation and these fellows can assist you. Old uncle," he added, addressing the family patriarch, "you will be glad to assist us, eh?" The old man nodded, agreeing less, Volkov suspected, from eagerness to aid the law than to avoid antagonizing someone powerful. "And, Mitka, you'd better hurry; it will be dark shortly. I shall take one guard and go to view the body, then return to headquarters and see if anyone has reported the girl missing. If not, I'll go home. Once it's dark, there's nothing more anyone can do. Report to me when you can."

During the ride to the house of the dead, Volkov became increasingly angry about the murders. "Heinous crimes", he kept repeating to himself. "If they continue, and where there are two there could be three, four---." He shuddered, the possibility of more looming ominously. "Why, they might disrupt the entire district." He arrived at his destination at the same time as Mitka's wife. "Ah, Yelena Dubova," he said addressing her, "it's good of you to come out to assist us. You know what it is about?"

"Yes, Luka told me. A sad business this, I don't know why such terrible things happen, Sudar." The small round woman was shaking her kerchiefed head in dismay. In the cold her plump cheeks were as rosy as apples and she was normally a cheerful soul but now her expression was bleak. After Luka helped her down from the horse which they'd been riding double, Volkov took her by the elbow and escorted her into the room where bodies found in the streets were laid out to be identified before burial.

An attendant, muffled against the cold in an array of patched and mismatched clothing, slowly shuffled forward. "The body of the young girl you've just received, where have you put it?" The man pointed to a bier just to the side of the entrance. Volkov lead the midwife to the body. He stepped aside and looked elsewhere in the cold and cheerless room, allowing her privacy for her examination. He heard her murmur, then give a sudden sharp exclamation. Her cry of protest was quickly followed by prayers for the dead, and she ended her outburst by heaping imprecations against the murderer.

The bailiff's wife approached Volkov and as she tugged at his sleeve, he turned to face her. She began to cry. Her normally upturned mouth was turned down in sorrow. "Eh, Yelena Dubova, I'm sorry you had to see this," said Volkov, gesturing towards the body, "but now I must ask you what you've discovered."

"No, no, my Lord, I know it must be done, but the girl was a virgin, an innocent, and yes, she was violated. There is blood there and on her thighs. You must find the devil that did this and punish him." She crossed herself as a protection against uttering the evil one's name.

"Can you tell me anymore about the girl? Her status perhaps? Her age?" Darya pulled a large handkerchief out of her sleeve and blew her nose but nodding she turned back to the body. He saw her pull down the girl's skirts, trying to give the child some semblance of dignity by smoothing her clothing. After a few moments of reflection she turned back to Volkov.

"It is as Luka said. The girl is, I would guess, about fifteen or sixteen years of age. Still at home with her parents, I should say, for she was a virgin and seems well taken care of as well. Indeed, one can see that at once. Notice here, my Lord, this neat darn in the elbow of her jacket and here in this stocking. And her clothes are warm and good. Or they were before she struggled with the fiend that did this.

"She could have had a tryst with some man," he ventured. Yelena Dubova shook her head.

"No, I think she was waylaid; I am sure she was an innocent. I pulled up her sleeves; her arms are bruised as well. And you can see that her clothing is torn." She demonstrated by indicating her own upper arms. "She must have been held in a tight grip for the bruises are quite evident."

"That it was a random encounter that ended in this tragedy, will make it the harder for us, you know," he said, softly.

She put her work-roughened hands up to her cheeks. "Yes, I know. Ah, her poor people whoever they are. This will be hard for them."

"Thank you, Yelena Dubova, for doing this for me. Luka will take you home and I will send Mitka back to you as soon as I am able." She nodded as Luka took her arm and led her away. Volkov turned to the attendant, tossing him a few dengi. "Keep this one until I tell you otherwise. She is sure to have people and they shall want to bury her properly." Volkov left, turned his horse towards his headquarters, disgusted with the human race in general and aware as well of the tentative beginnings of a headache. His general demeanor, when he arrived, cowed the clerks, who didn't dare for once even to pass a whisper among themselves.

Volkov sent one of his clerks to the nearest kabak for food and something to drink, the others he asked gruffly if anyone had reported a young girl missing.

They shook their heads in denial. And before the food arrived so did Mitka with a report on the results of his search at the site.

"Everything is done, but not a clue could we see and, Sudar, we used lanterns borrowed from the carters as well as our own. As to footprints or such like, the ground is frozen; there were none that we could see." Volkov's expression grew morose. "From her clothes, she seems a creature of little importance," said Mitka in an attempt to console his master.

"Everyone is important to someone," retorted Volkov. Shaken out of the complacency he'd felt at the first crime, he suddenly realized that he meant what he said.

46

CHAPTER FOUR

"A man and his wife have arrived, Sudar," announced one of the clerks late on the day following the murder. "They are reporting their daughter missing. She is about the right age for---." He gestured vaguely, leaving the rest unsaid.

"Then show them in." Volkov rose automatically as always, his height helping to intimidate those he questioned. The man and woman shown into the room were elderly, almost too old to have so young a child. Respectable folk from their dress, neat and warmly clad, though not wealthy by any means, the woman in plain dark voluminous skirts and a short heavy jacket with a fur hat over her kerchiefed head. An artisan of some sort, Volkov surmised, and so it proved to be, for the man was a baker by trade. The fellow was obviously frightened and kept twisting his cap in his hand and shuffling his boots. To a sheep, thought Volkov unkindly, every

48

official must seem a wolf. He turned his attention to the old woman and it was obvious she had been crying.

"So you want to report a missing daughter?"

"Yes, my Lord," ventured the old man.

"When did she vanish?"

"The day before yesterday."

"What time?" Volkov's sharp tone caused the old man to flinch. Softening his tone, he continued, "What time of day was it when she disappeared and under what circumstances? And how old was the girl?"

"Our Darya is just sixteen, my Lord. She didn't return from an errand."

"Weren't you alarmed at once?"

"We worried yes, but you see she'd gone with some bread to an elderly widow some streets away. The woman, Varvara Kusnetsova is alone and not too well. She has a good heart, our little Darya, and she often goes to help the widow. If it grows late, the widow often urges her to stay the night, for the companionship you see, and we thought it was so again. But the next morning when our Darya didn't return, I went to the widow myself and---." The old man's voice broke and his wife started crying softly.

"Sit," ordered Volkov. The couple timidly seated themselves on a bench pushed forward by the clerk. "Continue."

"The widow said my daughter left the evening before just when the sun was beginning to set. Then I knew something bad must have happened. Gosudar," said the old man, "she is a good girl and would come home to us if she were able. What could have happened to our Darya?" Volkov thought he knew and from his grim expression, the old people began to guess as well. "We searched the neighborhood, we went to every house and inquired, my old woman and I, but no one had seen her," continued the old man, his desperation evident in the sudden rush of his words. "So late, ordinary folk are eating their evening meal and preparing to go to bed. The roads must have been almost empty when Darya started back home."

"What was your daughter wearing?"

"A warm red jacket and a kerchief of the same color. She had her mittens and her warm felt boots. Her skirts were of a blue pattern."

"She is a neat girl," her mother spoke up, adding hopefully to the description.

"Then I am sorry but I have distressing news for you. Such a girl was found dead yesterday morning," and Volkov mentioned the neighborhood where she'd been found. The woman began to wail; the old man started to cry.

"She came to us late, my Lord," he said in broken tones, "our snow maiden. Like in the story of Snegurochka, she was the miracle of our old age. And like in the tale she has been lost to us." There was silence in the room while the old couple, both crying quietly, clung to one another.

During the interval, Volkov called to mind the old story to which Darya's father had referred. In the old tale an elderly childless couple out of their loneliness created a snowmaiden who was miraculously brought to life as a beautiful young girl. She became their loving child, a gift from God. But when spring came, she became sad and pale and melted away. The combined love of her adopted parents and of a young shepherd couldn't keep her by their side. Indeed, it was her response to that love, that doomed her.

Finally, the old man broke into Volkov's thoughts, "It was as we feared. Every dark thought entered our minds. Though we prayed and prayed that it would be otherwise." He stopped, and beginning again, asked softly, "How did our Darya die?"

"I am afraid she was murdered." The old man gave a despairing cry and put his arms around his wife who became to sob loudly. Volkov decided not to add that she'd been raped. They'll know soon enough, he thought, when the body was prepared for burial. He approached the couple and leaning closer said softly, "She is in a house of the dead. I will sign an order releasing her to you." He paused, finally asking, "How did you get here?"

"Someone brought us in a cart," whispered the old man through his tears.

"Is the fellow still here?" The old man shook his head. "Then I will send you there in one of our carts. You may use it to transport your daughter home and two of my men shall escort you." The old man stammered his thanks. Then still leaning close to one another for support, the bereft people followed the clerk out into the courtyard. After they'd gone Volkov bawled for Luka, who came running. "Go with them. Make absolutely sure the identification is correct." He paused to write an order and gave it to Luka, adding in a lower voice, "And show the poor souls every courtesy." Luka saluted, then hurried after the couple. Volkov kicked the door shut after him. He sat down in a foul mood and the clerks avoided him as much as possible for the remainder of the day.

When Mitka arrived, Volkov gave him the latest information, ordering him to go at once and question all the girl's neighbors, the widow as well, and the parents if possible. "Find out if there is someone these folk might suspect of such a crime. See if the girl had anyone that was bothering her with his attentions." He paused, deciding on further moves, then said, "Tomorrow, check with magistrates in the other districts and ask if any crimes of a similar nature have been reported. And that is about all we can do." He ran his hand over a list in front of him. "There are thefts, malicious mischief, and brawls as well that must concern us. Advent indeed," he grumbled. "And Ivan Andreyevich thinks it must be more peaceful because of the fast. The only sloth our citizens show is certainly not in the area of crime." He suddenly felt a strong urge to go out to a kabak for a drink, then decided instead to end his official day and eat and drink instead in the peace and comfort of his own home with his family around him.

Riding into his own courtyard, Volkov dismounted, handing the reins to one of his servants. He noticed a strange cart surrounded by servitors he didn't recognize. "Sofya has a visitor I see," he murmured, a discovery that did not improve his temper. He wanted peace, quiet, and his food, and the visitor, whoever it was, gone from the premises. When a maid opened the door to the vestibule, he caught sight of his wife through the door into the hall whispering to another woman already veiled and ready to leave. As Volkov strode into the room, the woman slipped out.

"Your food will be ready in a few moments," said Sofya, at once gauging Volkov's mood from his sour expression. She ordered the servants to take his coat and boots, then turning back to Volkov, urged, "Sit down and rest easy, Serezhenka."

"Who was your visitor?" he demanded.

"Irina Voronin." He grumbled but was mollified when at his wife's direction, one of menservants handed him a cup brimming with mead.

"She certainly stayed late; it's almost dark. Her husband should know better than to let her wander about at this hour."

"It's true that she arrived somewhat late in the day but she had news and wanted very much to share it with me."

"Gossip rather."

"You do Irina an injustice," protested Sofya. Volkov didn't bother to reply; he was too busy breaking bread and dipping it into the steaming bowl of soup that had been placed in front of him. Sofya sat down and taking bread herself, joined her husband in eating without, however, taking her eyes from him. Volkov looked up and saw her cautious expression.

We have a good relationship, he thought, and Sofya doesn't deserve to be snarled at the minute I step in the door. He added by way of explanation, "We've had a second murder and her people identified her today. It was another like the first."

"So that is the reason for your unhappy expression."

"And because God only knows if we'll ever catch

the fellow. There's nothing to tell us who it was unless some of the girl's neighbors reveal a suspect. Her parents are elderly, too, and have no other children. The poor souls, they were clothed in a black shroud of sorrow and I had to ladle out to them a drink filled with rue," he said, paraphrasing the words of an old song. "They said she was a late child, a blessing given them by God." Sofya's mouth turned down. She looked ready to shed tears of her own. "We shall do the best we can to bring the murderer to justice. If he attempts to flee, I shall track him like a wolf." Volkov reached for Sofya's hand and thought how attractive she looked in her blue sarafan and in a blouse embroidered with her own neat stitches. Her fair hair curled out from its confinement under a kerchief and he was tempted as always to twine the tendrils around his fingers. He suddenly felt a frisson of fear for her and it brought with it an even greater understanding of what young Darya's parents must have felt. Seeking to lighten the mood, he ventured to say, "Surely at least Irina was the bearer of happier news?" He waited but his wife chose not to be more forthcoming instead her mouth curved back up into a smile. There was an air of mischief about her now. "What are you thinking, little one? You have donned a most secretive smile."

"Oh, it is nothing, nothing at all, Serezhenka."

"Ah, a woman's heart is a dark forest, who can penetrate it," said Volkov, smiling at her.

Sofya Volkova, you are welcome indeed," Irina greeted her friend, following the salutation with a quick embrace and kiss on both cheeks. "Come and meet all

54

our dear friends." She leaned closer and whispered with a touch of mischief in her voice,

"We've been honored today by none other than the Boyarina Trubetskoya. Sofya, the woman actually sent a message asking to come when she heard from someone that the starets was to speak here today." Irina preened a bit at the success of her gathering while Sofya looked towards the stately woman her friend had named who was sitting in a position of solitary splendor near the stove. Intimidated by the high princely rank of her spouse, the other guests only ventured a few words and tentative smiles in that formidable woman's direction.

Glancing around the room, Sofya gave a brief nod to those she knew only slightly saving more enthusiastic waves and smiles for those who were her close friends. "Yes," continued Irina, "many of our Muscovite ladies would like to hear the famous starets who has come into our midst from far in the east but few have the courage to issue an invitation to him as I have done. With the sanction of my dear husband, of course, who heard him speak at the Shuisky residence. So, if these proud ladies wish to hear him, they must be nice to me."

Irina raised her hands to her face. "Oh, what am I thinking of, you haven't been allowed to sit down because I am babbling away as usual. Come, sit here," she said, walking in the direction of a cushioned seat, "and enjoy a bit of something to eat and drink."

"I don't see the starets."

"No, I asked him for a later hour. I thought we should eat, drink, and socialize before he arrived. It wouldn't do to disturb his preaching or whatever it is

exactly that he does. Here, Sofya, sit down next to Maria
Godunova. You know each other, yes? I will join you in
a few moments. I have to greet more guests," and she
fluttered ring-covered fingers in the direction of the door
to the women's quarters which had been opened by one
of a maids for the new arrivals. "And I really must see to
ordering more mead and cakes for everyone.
Unfortunately since it's Advent, most austere cakes
indeed."

Dropping her voice to a whisper, she added for
Sofya's ear only, "I had better say a few words to the
great Boyarina as well for she seems a bit lonely," and
left for the side of that august noblewoman.

So Sofya smiled, ready to strike up a
conversation with Maria Godunova with whom she was
slightly acquainted and against whom she didn't hold the
fact that she was the daughter of Malyuta Skuratov, one
of the Tsar's most loyal but most brutal henchman,
happily now deceased. Of more interest was that Maria
was married to Boris Godunov, who had only lately been
created a boyar and become a close advisor to the tsar on
foreign affairs. And about whom she had heard nothing
untoward.

But it was Maria Godunova who spoke first,
"Sofya Volkova, you're husband is a magistrate I
believe?"

"Yes, in the Belgorod district."

"My husband has spoken well of him." This came
as a surprise for the status of the Godunovs was now
very high indeed. Though, thought Sofya, their origins
are really rather humble. It was rumored there was even
a touch of the Tatar in their blood. As for Shuratov, he'd

been nothing until the tsar began to favor him. Maria gave her a friendly smile and Sofya chided herself for her unkind thoughts. "I do hope," said Maria, "that we will not have hell-fire and damnation flung at us today. If it is," she continued after a sip of mead, "I know I shall never be able to sleep tonight."

Sofya agreed with a nod. "You're right, but my Sergey heard him speak and remarked on the mildness of his sermonizing and surely since we are purported to be the more fragile species we will not have pictures of everlasting torment presented to us."

Maria looked skeptical. "But so many of them like to preach on the perfidy of women and add the torment and damnation as a fitting punishment."

Irina approached and overhearing their comments, seated herself next to them, adding, "And I do hope Otyets Yakov will avoid the ever popular theme of the daughters of Eve. I am tired of being accused of rebelliousness, gossiping, vanity, pertness, even lewdness." Since as she spoke, Irina looked decidedly pert and rebellious both Maria and Sofya laughed.

"And to be told time after time that we must be submissive, silent, and practice decorum," contributed Sofya, "is equally annoying."

"It is the monks, writing in their cells that put us in such a wicked light," hissed Irina. "What can they know of women."

"Well," laughed Sofya, "surely they had mothers. Sisters too."

"Ah, Sofya, you know very well what I mean. They are celibate and yet they pontificate about marriage. Moreover, I refuse to acknowledge that my very existence is an occasion of sin." In her indignation she'd raised her voice and the other women stopped their chatter, looking over in surprise. "Oh dear," whispered Irina, "I really must take care of what I say. Cakes or mead anyone," she loudly asked the company at large.

"When will this starets arrive?" asked one of the younger women.

"Soon, my dear. I wanted us to eat and drink first, for his sermon will no doubt be solemn and we wouldn't want to appear foolish in his eyes."

"Will he be able to cure my headaches? I have heard he has only to lay his hands on one's forehead and look into one's eyes to relieve suffering."

"If he can do that, could he cure my poor eyes?" asked an older woman. "I should so love to see everything as clearly as I did in my youth."

"Please," replied Irina, her voice raising anxiously, "do not expect miracles today. I have not heard such things of Otyets Yakov." The older woman sighed. "Though he is said to soothe one's worries with his look and a word," she added as a consolation. "Perhaps after all, when he has spoken to us, we can ask him for help." The woman nodded at this small assurance and they all went back to conversing in their small groups.

"Sofya," asked Irina, making herself more comfortable at her friend's side, "what is your Sergey investigating now?" Maria Godunova looked surprised at the question but bent forward herself to catch Sofya's reply.

"Well," she finally answered, not without misgiving, "he is investigating two murders."

"Oh, murder, such a heinous crime. Does he have the culprits in hand? And who was it that was murdered?" asked the irrepressible Irina. In her eagerness for an answer, she betrayed her great interest in the crimes.

Again, after some hesitation and in greatly lowered tones, Sofya gave Irina the information she sought. "First a maidservant, then a very young girl." Maria Godunova at once expressed her horror and appeared genuinely shocked. How ironic, thought Sofya, that the daughter of the tsar's most vicious tool against suspected boyars and their wives and children, expresses such repugnance over these two murders. Does she really not know how feared and hated her father was? And that nursemaids still frightened wicked little boys by telling them that Skuratov would come and carry them off if they didn't behave?

"The young girl what class was she?" Sofya saw fear on the face of both women and an eagerness to hear that they and theirs were in no danger from some murdering fiend.

"The only child of an elderly couple. The father is a baker. Sergey feels quite badly for them." Both Maria and Irina quickly expressed sympathy for the bereaved parents.

"What happened to the poor child?" pressed Irina, reassured now as to her own safety and still eager to learn the details.

"Oh, it was a terrible way to die, Irina," said Sofya, then stopped but her friend waited for more. "She was raped and strangled." She spoke so softly, her two companions barely heard her reply.

Irina finally had the information that she wanted and now seemed sorry she'd taken her questions so far. She plucked nervously at her skirts. "Perhaps after all, it is good that we are so closely protected and not forced to wander in the streets like the women of lower class. But surely your man will catch the criminal responsible?"

"I don't know," Sofya blurted out, feeling most uncomfortable. She was relieved when the starets was announced and Irina's attention was drawn to him. Sofya noticed that he arrived with a servant to whom she took an immediate dislike for he seemed disdainful of all of them. "Why is he glaring at us?

I'm sure we've done nothing to offend him," she whispered to Maria who shrugged in response. The fellow took his master's cloak, was shown into a corner of the room, and with her back to him, Sofya didn't have to be bothered with his intimidating expressions any longer and so promptly forgot him.

"This is Otyets Yakov; he has come to speak to us," announced Irina, somewhat superfluously. Turning to the starets, she added, "We are so grateful that you could come. Let me offer you some bread and salt. And will you eat and drink something first? What is your pleasure?"

"Good wives, mothers, daughters, thank you for inviting me. And, yes, I will take a bit of refreshment first," he said, bowing slightly to his hostess. Irina immediately ordered a small table to be placed at his side then that food and something to drink be put there as well. To Sofya's relief, her friend's duties to her primary guest kept her fluttering around the starets. Trying to push thoughts of the murder aside, she concentrated instead on the person of the starets. Dark among our gay colors, he looks like a carrion crow lost in a crowd of blooms, she thought. Why, he's quite common and unattractive. But as she continued to examine the man, she noted the grace of his gestures and the luminosity of his dark eyes. His deep, rich voice, too, was quite reassuring and she decided after a few moments of thought to give him her approval.

Having eaten a little, the starets declared himself satisfied and rose to speak. Everyone gave him their full attention. He began his sermon with a passage from Proverbs. "Who will find a capable wife? Her worth is beyond price." The starets went on to speak of the duties attendant on being a good wife, adding finally, "If she does all the things of which I have spoken, then as the holy book says, a good wife will be her husband's joy."

"I have heard all these things," thought Sofya, "but he makes them sound so right that I'm sure we will take them to heart."

The starets reminded them that Christ had been born of a woman and she had been submissive to her Lord. "What better example of a good woman can we have than this?" There was a respectable silence at the end of his sermon and he concluded by blessing them all.

"Is there any further way," he asked, "in which I can assist you."

Irina spoke up. "Several of the women are troubled by physical ailments. Would it be too great a trouble? I mean, can you perhaps help them?"

"With faith anything is possible even through such a humble instrument as myself. I am, by our own dear Lord, permitted to be of some small assistance in this way. But who is it among you that is troubled?" The woman with the headaches spoke up. The starets approached her and placed his hand on her forehead, rather awkwardly because of her headdress. Finally cupping her face in his hands, he tilted her face towards his. "Look at me and pray with me, my sister in Christ." The woman clasped her hands in an attitude of prayer and concentrated her gaze upon his eyes as he gently rubbed her forehead with his long fingers. Sofya looked on in wonder for the woman seemed totally entranced by the starets. Finally her eyes closed and when he stopped his ministrations there was a peaceful smile on her face.

"Is there anyone else," he said very softly, "that could use my humble services?"

"Varvara Lobanova's sight is failing, Otyets," ventured Irina.

"Ah, for such a miracle one must have a faith that can move mountains. But lead me to the lady and perhaps I can soothe her spirit, so that she understands that seeing with her soul the good of the Lord is more important than seeing the things of this world with her eyes. We will pray with her." And they did and tears coursed down Varvara's cheeks and to Sofya they appeared to be tears of joy. He went on to speak to several more women and put his hands upon them and they all seemed the better for it.

At last the visit came to an end and the starets and his servant departed. All the women agreed that he was a most impressive man, a good man, even a saintly man. "I shall have something to tell Serezhenka," thought Sofya. "It's strange that he told me so very little about the starets and even that little seemed reluctantly expressed." Then still moved by the afternoon's events, she left for home.

CHAPTER FIVE

Slightly out of patience, Volkov watched as the five elders bowed repeatedly and in unison heaped fulsome praise and blessings on him. Finally satisfied that the magistrate bore them no ill-will, their spokesman stepped forward. He removed his fur-trimmed hat, revealing a bowl-shaped cap of neatly trimmed short white hair, but despite an open mouth he still hesitated to speak. Volkov finally gestured for him to proceed. "Sudar," the fellow began, and in spite of his obsequious tone Volkov thought that with his white hair and long flowing beard he resembled nothing so much as a dignified Biblical patriarch, "we feel that justice has been served and—." Volkov had a busy day ahead of him and bracing himself wondered if the fellow was about to launch into a long and tedious speech but the elder kept his thanks within reason.

"Yes, yes, I shall see to it that this fellow is

64

punished. The miscreant has repeated his crimes and I deem him utterly unrepentant. However he shall have considerable difficulty assaulting honest Christians and thieving from them minus a hand." Again the chief elder and his companions nodded with satisfaction.

"As it wisely said, fear not the law but the judge, eh, Sudar?" Volkov gave them all a thin smile, accepted additional murmurs of gratitude and gestured that they might leave. But as the elder hesitated, Volkov impatiently ordered him to say what he had to say. "It has come to our ears. That is, people have been talking. Our wives and daughters you understand, Sudar---." He paused to take a deep breath while Volkov fumed. "We are all worried about this fiend who is going about murdering women in our district."

Volkov clenched his fists. I knew this would make trouble, he thought. "Be reassured we are investigating both murders. Nor are they necessarily related. Indeed, both are undoubtedly the work of acquaintances of the young women in question. There is nothing for you to fear personally. But that is not to say that you may become careless with your womenfolk and maidservants. It is your duty to supervise their comings and their goings. Is that not so?" The elders all nodded. "Then do your duty and your womenfolk will be safe. And I promise you that the murderers will be brought to justice." They elders looked relieved and so Volkov motioned them to go. As they bowed their way out, Mitka attempted to thrust his way in and between the bailiff's stockiness and the chief elder's paunch, it was some moments before both managed to extract themselves. Volkov smiled at his chief lieutenant who was gasping like a fish out of water.

"You are obviously the bearer of important tidings."

"I just heard something important that concerns us." He looked around taking in Volkov, the clerks, the guard; even the logs of the wall it seemed were to be included in his concern.

"What is it?"

"It happened in the Skorodom."

"That's not our district. How could what happened there possibly concern us?"

"But it does," Mitka insisted.

"Then tell us what happened." As usual Mitka was drawing the matter out far more than necessary. He even turned slightly to see if the clerks were listening. They were and didn't have to strain themselves to hear for Mitka's carrying voice reached them quite clearly.

"As you will see, it is clearly of great importance to us."

Sometimes Volkov felt like a midwife officiating at an especially difficult birth. He sighed. "Mitka, you are like a hen guarding its eggs. Shall we hear these details before night falls?"

Mitka was put off his stride by this last remark and the clerks sniggered but he quickly recovered and after a suitably pregnant pause, announced, "Another murder, Sudar." Again there was a pause. "Just like ours and it happened last night or early this morning," he finished with a rush. He looked around with satisfaction, having finally delivered his news.

"But in the Skorodam?" Mitka nodded vigorously. "Is this just a rumor or did you actually go there and speak to the officials in charge?"

"Oh, it's a fact, Sudar. When I heard, I went at once to the magistrate's headquarters and interviewed his bailiff. It seems a young girl was raped and strangled in the same manner as our victim and then left to decorate the front of a church. The priest found her this morning on his way to say Mass and that poor soul is still addled by his discovery."

"Have they any more clues than we had?"

"None that I know of."

"We shall have to find out. I'll leave it to you." Volkov thought about the matter a further few moments, at last adding, "The murders occurred after the barriers were down. Either the Skorodom crime is not related or this murderer roams freely. Perhaps he changes his dwelling frequently and how is that possible?" Volkov looked puzzled. After a pause, he asked, "How is your own questioning going? Have the baker's neighbors and this widow given you any useful information?"

"No, not a thing, Sudar. The poor old widow wrings her hands, calls on the Lord and His Blessed Mother but adds nothing to our knowledge of the crime. As to the neighbors, all the young men and the old ones too for that matter, are, it seems, upright Christians and models of good behavior and—," Mitka's expression grew lugubrious, "everyone seems to be accounted for at the critical time."

"No one courting the girl?"

"To be sure there were some suitors, but it was families seeking a bride for their sons. No lad's been sighing at her gate. Nor did young Darya ever report anything of that sort, that is, someone importuning her, to her parents. No, there is no one in the vicinity known for being rapacious."

"And what of your first investigation. Anything new there?'

"No, I'm afraid not. Sudar, the men tell me they are anxious for their women. I expect they will be escorted on their errands and held as close as any boyarina until this evil fellow is apprehended."

"I think that perhaps the murderer saw an opportunity for rape, seized it, then covered his tracks. So it would actually be better if the women were guarded as carefully as sheep from a wolf. Mitka, see if this Skorodom murder could have been done by the same fellow."

"I shall speak to Vanka Maleev, that is, to the Magistrate's bailiff. I'll have him keep me abreast of their investigation."

"If their murder was done by the same fellow, we could have more of these crimes." Volkov's expression changed from one of puzzlement to one of disgust. "I have heard of such things elsewhere; we may have a fiend with a taste for this sort of thing and it could continue." Mitka crossed himself. Thinking about the elders, Volkov added, "There is always the possibility that if our citizens become frightened enough, they will see this evil fellow behind every bush and cause numbers of innocent men to be apprehended. I have seen such panics myself." He sat back, and in the ensuing silence, his thoughts drifted to the finger pointing some years ago when the slightest suspicion and flimsiest accusations of treason could sentence a man to death. Thank the Lord, he thought, that now the law is more closely observed. Volkov looked up to see Mitka still hovering and abruptly rose himself. "Let this other business wait," he said, indicating a mound of rolled and bound papers on his desk. "A murder inquiry should take precedence and we still have a few hours before dark. I shall ride with you. Magistrate Pugachev is an old friend. He will tell me what he knows. You shall speak to Maleev, find out the details from him and take the time to view the body yourself. Call out two guards only to accompany us," he ordered and Mitka nodded.

The ride to the Skorodom district was made in better time than Volkov expected. The bitter cold had almost cleared the thoroughfares. "Ah, Sudar, no crowds to impede our progress," shouted Mitka from his position next to Volkov. "The icy fingers of Father Frost have driven our citizens into their own cozy homes." Volkov felt shivers of cold himself, and picturing the men and women of Moscow installed in front of their stoves basking in the warmth, he, for a moment, envied them. Then remembering the business that had brought him out into the cold, he pressed his lips together in determination and urged on his horse.

"Welcome to my headquarters," called out Pugachev when he saw the party of four ride into the courtyard of his headquarters. Striding over to Volkov, he embraced his old acquaintance, then tugging at his sleeve pulled him inside a warm and comfortable room. "Mead here at once," he ordered of a waiting servant. "And heat it up, you lazy good for nothing, my good friend here looks frozen. Come, Volkov, you can shed one layer at least." After a clerk took Volkov's mittens and outer coat, Pugachev led him to a bench near the stove. Volkov rubbed his hands together, receiving the warm mug gratefully and using it to warm himself still further. "Even farts freeze on a day like this," said Pugachev, laughing. Volkov nodded and began sipping his mead. He saw Mitka seek out his counterpart and they retreated together to another corner of the room. Pugachev looked at them, then back to his guest. "You've come about this murder, I suppose? Your bailiff made a big to-do about it when he burst in here this morning. Thinks we have the same fellow going about strangling girls in every district. No, no, friend, it can't be the same fellow. Look close to home, I say, and that is what I intend to do." He put a finger to the side of a nose that was almost obscured by his bush of a mustache. "It was some rascally acquaintance of the girl's but we shall find him out." He gave a snort. "She probably brought it on herself. After all if a bitch doesn't want it and won't hold still, then how can the dog possibly mount?" He laughed. "Yes, close to home is the answer. It's where we'll look and you'd best do the same."

"Unfortunately we have no suspects. The neighborhood of our deceased young women contains only fine, upstanding Christians."

Pugachev chortled. "Is there such a species?" Then his amusement turned into a frown. "There is a great deal of wickedness abroad and it is only fear that keeps our worthy citizens from larcenous behavior." He jabbed a finger into the air to make his point. "Fear of damnation, but even better, for the rascals don't think that far ahead, fear of the knout and the hangman's noose is what makes them exercise caution, eh?" He tilted his head to one side and held up a hand as if it were tightening a noose.

Volkov made an effort not to let his annoyance over Pugachev's oversimplification of the murders show. No use, he thought, antagonizing him when one wants information. "Have you any clues, footprints leading somewhere or the like."

"Footprints, footprints, you say? Oh, we have no shortage of those. The priest's screams brought out his entire family and others in the neighborhood as well; the scene of the crime was well-trodden with footprints before we got to the site. No, we shall not find the murderer that way. Instead my bailiff shall interview all those close to the girl."

"You've identified her then?"

"Yes, someone recognized her." He shuddered. "Not that she was at her best. We shall have this fellow." He slapped his hand against the arm of his chair. "Ah, Volkov, if only our Muscovites were meek and humble. Still, it is our job to keep them that way. Yes, with fear, as I told you. A little trembling won't hurt them. At any rate they are used to suffering. He who says Moscow does not believe in tears speaks the truth."

"Your notion reminds me of a preacher I just heard. He says meekness is the character we must all assume. Further, this starets insists that suffering is the way to salvation."

"See, it is as I told you. I agree entirely," he laughed heartily again, "as long, of course, as it others who do the suffering." Then he tilted his head to the side and affected a serious air. "I believe I have heard of this fellow you mention. He is in demand everywhere. They say that the Metropolitan has made a pet of him and has him dining in splendor at his palace. Yes, worthies are falling all over themselves to invite the fellow to sup and sermonize. I hear he heals as well. A bit of a miracle-worker. And you say you've heard him?"

"Yes, and I must admit I was impressed with his words." That he was somewhat repelled by the man personally, Volkov chose not to tell Pugachev.

"I believe I should like to hear this fellow myself," said Pugachev. "Now as to this murder," he continued, changing the subject once again, "to be sure, I will keep you apprised of what we discover. Meanwhile your bailiff can see what we saw." The magistrate shuddered again. "A desecration of church property, I say, though it was probably an accident of circumstances rather than a statement against religion. These crimes are really all quite simple when it comes down to it, one mustn't read all manner of unusual motives into them."

"No doubt you're right. Yet all the victims were left beside holy places."

"Coincidence." Pugachev waved his fingers in a dismissive gesture and Volkov shrugged in reply. He began to think he was wasting his time, and starting to feel hunger pangs, decided to end his day and go straight home. Pugachev noted his downcast looks and added, "You worry too much, Volkov, remember no fox is so clever he doesn't get caught in the end."

"I'll leave my Mitka to finish questioning your man. As for myself, I'm for home." His stomach suddenly growled and both men laughed.

"Yes, you'd best be on your way, home to watery mushroom broth and turnip pie." He snorted. "We're eating like peasants. Ah, I tell you, my friend, when the Christmas feast finally begins I shall indulge in meat pies without number and blini richly covered in cream." He smacked his lips. "Let the domovoy have the pickled beets and groats, I say. Though if that is all he gets, he'll shower no blessings on us." Volkov laughingly agreed.

Giving Pugachev his thanks and good wishes, Volkov left for home with one of the two guards. In his own vestibule he was assailed by various tantalizing aromas and grinned in anticipation. But after shedding coat, hat, mittens, and changing his boots for soft shoes, he was chagrined to discover that most of the delicious smells belonged to cakes and sauces, condiments and meads, that were being prepared in advance of the holiday season.

"You mean," he grumbled to Sofya, "that none of these enticing aromas will go on the table tonight?"

"Ah, Serezhenka, you know we must start Christmas brewing and baking early. I want to set a fine table for all the folk that will be coming to share with us. A fine mistress I would be, if I left everything until the last moment. Today, we've been brewing extra kvass for the servants and honey mead with spices for us. We've even poured honey over the Kuzmin apples. The men have been cleaning and I sent them out for fresh pine boughs. Look around you, already the rooms are taking on a festive air. And it shall get even more hectic the closer Christmas comes. Besides it is still Advent and you must fast."

Looking at her as she stood arms akimbo, Volkov thought Sofya seemed pleased rather than harassed by all the work that she contemplated. And since he was being

73

served his dinner, he gave up his injured air and settled down to filling his belly. He commented approvingly on all the preparations. "My favorite time of year, little one, I shall look forward to all the good things that it brings."

"Nor has today been only work for I have Matryona to supervise the maids and she does it to my satisfaction." Abruptly she seated herself and leaning towards Volkov with an air of excitement, said, "I went to Irina's home today. There were other ladies there. We heard the starets preach. Yes, he came just for us today," she added proudly. Volkov was suddenly and immeasurably annoyed, so much so that it put him off his food. He put down his spoon and frowned at his wife who was staring at him with an air of self-satisfaction.

"He spoke to you alone in the women's quarters?"

"Serezhenka, there were twenty of us, that is hardly being alone and besides he is a holy man. Why, the Metropolitan is sponsoring him. Otyets Yakov told what an honor it was, this recognition of his humble services." Volkov thought sourly that there was nothing humble about the man except for a few affected mannerisms. "Surely you were impressed with the starets yourself, so what possible objection can you have to our hearing him too? Didn't you say that Ivan Andreyevich allowed him to see his wife and felt that the starets had done her a great deal of good? So why object to my hearing him as well?"

It was difficult for Volkov to explain his ambivalent attitude towards the starets but knew that he didn't like the idea of that fellow in the same room with Sofya. He shook his head. "I believe I would have forbidden your attendance had I known what you were planning."

"But," spluttered Sofya, "you told me you were impressed by his sermon."

"With his words yes, not with his person. There is something deceptive about the fellow. Somehow his presence in a roomful of women reminds me of a weasel in a henhouse," he blurted out. "A wolf in sheep's clothing that is what he is."

Sofya laughed. "What a silly notion. You sound petulant and jealous." She noted his immediate stormy look and sought to mollify him. "Why he never laid a hand on us," then ruined the effect she was striving for by blushing. At once Volkov narrowed his eyes. "Well, one cannot count the fact that he placed his hand on our foreheads, that is those who suffered from headaches, and others, why it is true he grasped their hands, but it was only to soothe and reassure. Why even prim and pious Olga found no objection to his touch." She finally noticed that the more she said the angrier Volkov's countenance grew until at last he slapped a hand on the table for silence.

"I don't want you to attend any more sessions with this fellow, do you hear? If the other husbands are such fools as to allow it, let them suffer the consequences."

Sofya gave a toss of the head. "Well, I have more than enough to do because Christmas is drawing near but I still think you are being unfair to Father Yakov. I don't understand why you've taken against him, I really don't." Volkov looked past her shoulder into the corner of the room where candles were lit before the icons, wondering himself why he was being so unreasonable. It could be his past still intruding, he thought. "Perhaps, Serezhenka," added Sofya, determined to have the last word, "you are like the head of a wolf pack, afraid of competition from some other male. But the starets isn't some young man seeking to take your place. He is only a kind and holy man, preaching to us of God's goodness."

Volkov slammed down his mug breaking it into a dozen pieces, startling both of them. Instantly regretting his loss of control, he chided himself for being a fool, remembering that even if a man has no good days, he can still have good nights. He mumbled an apology of sorts to Sofya. She nodded but nonetheless regarded him with wariness for the rest of the evening.

CHAPTER SIX

The following day Volkov decided to lay to rest the worm that was gnawing at him. "I shall simply find out more about this starets and that knowledge will hopefully allay my suspicions. Yet what a fool I am," he grumbled, as he restlessly paced up and down in the courtyard of his home while his horse was being saddled. "Have I nothing better to do then to chase after--. Ah, as well try to discover the elusive bannik in the bathhouse or hope to catch the domovoy when he comes to feed." His mumbled self-doubts caused his waiting escort to turn in his direction. Seeing the curious glance, Volkov tightened his lips as he mounted and turned his horse, not in the direction of his headquarters but towards the Shuisky estate.

"I shall interview the chaplain," he thought. He laughed bitterly, which caused an expression of confusion to cross his guard's face, but Volkov, now thoroughly wrapped up in his own thoughts, failed to notice. "Yes, question a man whom I caught giving the starets an envious look. What can he have to say that would relieve me? I should ride to the Metropolitan's palace and speak to the staff there instead. Of course, they will have nothing but good reports about the man or he wouldn't have been given their protection. Nor would they welcome my suspicions. Why, they would ask, are you inquiring? And what could I say? That I don't like Father Yakov's looks? A fool's errand indeed."

At the Shuisky gate, Volkov was informed that Ivan Petrovich and his sons were all at the Kremlin. When he announced that he only wished to see the chaplain, the gatekeeper opened one of the large wooden doors of the gate and admitted him, bawling loudly at the same time for someone to see to the magistrate's horse. One among the numerous members of the staff, many of whom were idly standing about with nothing better to do than stare curiously at anything of interest, helped him dismount and took the reins. Still another servant escorted Volkov into the empty hall where a waiting attendant took his coat, hat, and mittens. The fellow left to find the chaplain and until he could be found, Volkov warmed himself by the huge stove.

"You wished to see me, Magistrate?" asked the priest when he finally arrived. Volkov nodded. "What can I do for you?" He tilted his head to one side, his expression and stance both implying puzzlement as to why he in particular should have been sought out for an interview. Dressed in a rusty black garment, his scraggly grey hair barely contained under a black hat, he was as dour a fellow as Volkov remembered.

"May we sit, Father?"

"Of course, Magistrate, of course," replied the priest in some haste, remembering his manners at last. "I shall order something to warm you, hot spiced mead will no doubt be welcome after the bitter cold outdoors." From the bulky redness of his nose, thought Volkov, the fellow warmed himself the year round on mead. "I'm sure Ivan Petrovich would want me to see that you're made comfortable," continued the priest. Volkov said hot mead would be appreciated and the priest ordered for the two of them. After a few sips of the mead and an equally few comments on the forthcoming Christmas festivities, Volkov leaned closer, finally coming to the purpose for his visit.

"I've come to learn more about this Father Yakov. Surely as a fellow cleric you can answer my questions about this most interesting fellow. I was quite impressed when I heard him speak but know nothing of his background."

The chaplain sniffed rather haughtily, replying, "Father is only a courtesy title. He is not an ordained priest. Nor is he a member of the regular clergy." He seemed pleased to be able to report the tenuous relationship of the starets to holy orders. "He is not affiliated with any monastery though some of them have sanctioned his preaching."

The chaplain doesn't seem at all surprised by my inquiries, perhaps, thought Volkov, because the starets is rightly an object of curiosity. "Where was he before he arrived here in the capital?"

"I believe he preached and healed in Nizhni Novgorod."

"Is that his place of origin?"

"No, I think he is from Perm or from some other remote and barbarous place on the eastern frontier." The chaplain looked at Volkov, somewhat puzzled by the questions.

"So far away. From the frontier you say?"

"Yes, and he says his origins are humble."

"Tell me, what is your opinion of this man?" The chaplain's expression grew guarded but Volkov leaned still closer, inwardly shuddering as he encountered the man's dank smell. He narrowed his eyes to make his presence more intimidating, suspecting the chaplain was a timorous sort. In fact, noted Volkov, the fellow's looking a mite apprehensive.

"Why," the priest stammered, "the starets is a good and holy man. The Metropolitan has approved his presence here in Moscow. He is received everywhere. What else can I say about him?" Now the chaplain appeared confused. "I have not been in his presence that often. I've only met him here on a few occasions."

"And you formed no opinion? Tell me do you trust the man?"

"Why I---. Why, I suppose so. Has he done something wrong? Is that why you are inquiring?" The chaplain bent towards Volkov and there was a touch of avidity in his last question.

Volkov placed his hands firmly on the table, looked sternly at the priest and declared, "I am a magistrate. I must make these inquiries. We wouldn't want a fraud imposing on us, would we?"

"No, no, of course not."

"So, to put it bluntly did you see anything at all in

the behavior of this starets that might mark him as a fraud?" Taking liberties, he hinted, "Certain parties are interested." Volkov could read the chaplain's thoughts from the changing expressions on his face and almost laughed. The priest was drawing the desired conclusion. An officer of the law, suspicions, and inquiries, smacked of palace doings. And the chaplain knew of Volkov's ties to the palace because of the successful conclusion to a previous murder investigation in which both the Grand Prince and his employers, the Shuiskys, had had an interest. He added, "I assure you this will go no further. I am merely making inquiries in the interests of the law." It was obvious that the chaplain would now do his best to help Volkov.

"Well, Sudar, I can't really like the fellow for all his talents at preaching and healing. He and that fellow of his treated me as of no account. He was not so abrupt with my mistress and her ladies, I can tell you. There it was all sweet honeyed words and he had the temerity to lay his hands on them. I would never presume to do such a thing. I think he took liberties under the guise of soothing them." His voice had dropped to a whisper even though no one was in the room with them, his tone full of indignation. His words were soothing to Volkov's ears even as the magistrate's conscience hinted that the words were only the result of envy and spite.

"Tell me more about Otyets Yakov's origins if you can."

"Well, he comes from the frontier as I've said. And he's as uncouth in manner as these Cossacks who've lately come to Moscow from there. He knows the fellows too. I heard him say so to the Master. Brigands is what those Cossacks are in spite of their victories over the Khan. Still I suppose one must give them some credit for defeating those infidel dogs." The last was said grudgingly. Volkov had found the chaplain timid and officious on the many occasions they'd met at the Shuisky manor but obviously he seethed with opinions which now came pouring out. "And, I say, what good is such a fellow if he consorts with brigands?"

"You mean the starets?" The chaplain nodded.

"He drinks like a fish too. I've seen him do it. And did not Vassily, of blessed memory, preach to us all how it is seemly to abstain from drunkenness." He paused. "Though I must admit he can hold his drink. A sly fellow indeed." Obviously, thought Volkov, the fellow considers it was more reprehensible for the starets to remain in control of his faculties when drinking heavily than to quietly lie down on the table and go to sleep as many Muscovites were wont to do. The chaplain whispered, "Perhaps he is in league with the evil one and his healing and preaching are a devilish ruse." He stopped to cross himself.

"Can you tell me anymore?" The chaplain pondered a few moments then shook his head. His demeanor became apprehensive, as if he'd said too much and he slid away from Volkov, further down the bench. Quickly, Volkov reassured him. "This will go no further. We will keep it between us, eh?" The chaplain agreed at once, sighing with relief. Volkov rose to go and the chaplain blessed him and saw him to the door. "If anyone asks why I was here, why I came to you for some advice as one does come to priests, eh? Which is true in a manner of speaking." The chaplain nodded.

Volkov rode to his headquarters still dissatisfied. He'd gotten what he wanted but it seemed of little worth coming as it did from an envious colleague and consisting as it did of hearsay and rumor. "Something I knew before I asked the first question." He snorted. "Nor have I stilled my worm."

Mitka was waiting for him at headquarters, so Volkov asked, "Anything new in our murder inquiries?"

"I believe that all three killings were done by the same evil fiend but Magistrate Pugachev and his bailiff are skeptical. "We are still questioning folk here; they are still investigating there." Mitka shrugged. "What more can anyone do?"

"Is there anything else you have to report?"

"No, Sudar."

"Then I'll get to the other matters waiting for my attention." In the early afternoon, after a good three hours work, Volkov left with Mitka for the nearest kabak only to find that a ruckus had broken out. With difficulty making their way on horseback through the crowds of curious bystanders, it was some moments before they reached the front of the kabak.

"Like pigs at a trough," commented Mitka, after shouting at the onlookers to let them pass. Surrounded by his staff, they saw the host standing outside his establishment wringing his hands. He ran up to Volkov as soon as he saw him.

"You came quickly, Magistrate, thanks the Lord." His tones turned into a wail. "They are making a shambles of my kabak. Everything is being broken. My mead is all spilt." Volkov could hear loud cries as well as other ominous sounds from inside the place. Every vulgarism in the language was being hurled about in addition to the furniture and crockery. One of the kabak's waiters was sitting on an upturned barrel nursing a bloody head. Another, still in one piece, Volkov signaled to hold his horse after he'd dismounted.

"Who are they?"

"Those brigands, the Cossacks. The fiends chased out all my regular customers. They grew angry because we didn't serve them fast enough." The host seized Volkov by his sleeve and clung fast even when the magistrate tried to shake him off. "You and your man must do something."

"Then let go of me, you fool. How many are there?"

"Five, Sudar, there are five of the fucking bastards."

"Mitka, ride back and get Luka and the guard at once." Mitka mounted and rode off as well as he could through the steadily growing crowd, while Volkov approached the door of the kabak. Just as he reached the entrance a mug came hurtling out and caught him a glancing blow. His heavy fur hat was knocked into the street and he staggered back. Touching his forehead he felt a trickle of blood and pulled out a handkerchief which he clapped over the cut. The host began commiserating with him.

"See, these brutes respect no one, Magistrate."

After Volkov recovered he moved forward with more caution. Reaching the door of the kabak, he shouted, "I order you to desist in the name of the law." He was greeted by unsavory comments on his ancestors. "Hey Cossacks, your Father the Tsar won't appreciate your spilling his taxes on the floor. Come out and make it easier on yourselves." Further drunken retorts were the only reply. By now, the street was packed from one side to the other with the curious, and Volkov had constantly to order them back. Calling out, they passed along their own comments on the situation, pleased at this diversion in an otherwise ordinary day. Even the cold didn't deter them. Vendors sensing business began to circulate among them. Volkov sighed and stood waiting for his guard while the host continued to lament over his losses. Oblivious to the excitement around them, a number of thin, unkempt fellows with sagging shoulders were leaning up against the kabak's walls.

"Drunkards, probably been there all morning," Volkov mused aloud, "hoping for a handout from someone." When he turned from staring at them, he saw Father Yakov making his way through the crowd. Following in his footsteps, like a small rowing boat drawn along in the wake of a more impressive barge, was his ever present disciple.

"What's amiss, Magistrate?"

"Five of these Cossacks that were welcomed by the city as heroes are in a drunken state and breaking up this poor fellow's establishment and spilling the devil knows how much good mead and vodka." The disciple and the host crossed themselves at mention of the devil. The starets only smiled.

"Ah, these fellows become so rowdy when the drink takes them. They can be short-tempered, crude, and rough. But, Magistrate, believe me, they are really good at heart. I know them; I can deal with them." He threw his cape to his disciple and started for the door.

Volkov seized him by the sleeve.

"Look at this fellow," he said pointing to the waiter still nursing his bloody head, "they could do the same to you."

"But they won't," replied the starets. Shaking off Volkov's restraining hand, he entered shouting, "Hey, sons of Yermak, good friends, it's Yakov here, your little father. Put away your arms; lay down your pots and stools. There are no Tatars here, only a few harmless Muscovites. Hey, hey, you're spilling good mead and vodka. Stop at once. What a waste, my friends."
The starets disappeared into the kabak and there was a sudden silence as the thuds and knocks and clatter ceased.

Into the quiet rode Mitka and the rest of Volkov's men. They dismounted, but Volkov stopped them from going any further. "What, what?" spluttered Mitka.

"Otyets Yakov, our visiting starets, has offered to subdue the fellows; it seems they're members of his flock. Let's wait and our job might be done for us. Save us a few broken heads." Mitka stared at the dried trickle of blood on Volkov's forehead and then down at the fur hat still lying in the street. Looking at his superior with a dubious expression, he stooped to pick it up. A few minutes later, the starets appeared in the doorway.

"Come in, Magistrate, my friends are like little lambs again." Volkov rather doubted this but entered anyway, treading his way among the broken bits of furniture and puddles of spilled spirits, the anxious host still on his coattails. The Cossacks, in various stages of drunkenness and subdued truculence, were all sitting or standing around the starets. The host shrieked when he saw the damage to the serving room and from behind the magistrate hurled imprecations at the offenders.

"Dogs of Tatars. Fucking brigands. Sons of bitches." One of the Cossacks made as if to rise. The starets motioned him down while the host hastily retreated to the doorway. From there he shouted, "Who will pay for all this? I will bring charges before this magistrate."

"They will pay," declared the starets. "They've been received in the palace, bells were rung in their honor only a few days ago. They are heroes, eh? A little disorder can surely be forgiven?"

"They won't be heroes long if they continue to destroy Muscovite property and spill Muscovite mead," retorted Volkov.

"Magistrate," replied the starets, holding out his hands in a gesture of entreaty, "these fellows are from the frontier, from the Volga some of them, they don't know how to behave in a civilized place. They are simply rowdy children. I personally promise that someone will pay."

"The bill will not be cheap. It isn't poor man's kvass they've spilt. This won't be reckoned in kopecks but in rubles."

"Yes, yes," agreed the host, almost apoplectic with rage, with his hair standing on end where he'd tugged at it in frustration.

"And there's the assault on the poor waiter."

"They tell me he insulted them," replied the starets mildly. "These are proud fellows and won't have their ancestors so rudely described. You'd be angry yourself at such an insult, eh, Magistrate?" Volkov

thought of the similar insults that had been hurled
through the doorway at him but merely shrugged.
Reminded of the waiter's insults, one of the biggest and
burliest of the Cossacks rose menacingly. "No, no,
Vannuska, sit down. No more temper." The starets
pointed to the man who had risen. "This is Ivan Koltso,
the chief lieutenant of Yermak Timofeyevich. The
very man entrusted with Kuchum Khan's treasure of furs
and news of the victory for the Tsar. Remember this is
the first real city these men have seen; they don't know
quite how to act."

"They need a keeper."

"And they've found one. I will be their surety."
The Cossacks grunted their approval.

Volkov turned to the host. "If they pay for
everything broken and spilt and compensate the waiter
for his broken head," and his voice rose over a protest
from Koltso, "will you be satisfied?"

The host gave it some thought and using a slate
he found on the floor began his reckonings. While he
waited, Volkov was surprised to see two of the Cossacks
put their heads down on a table and begin to snore. The
starets smiled. That man, thought Volkov, just saved me
and my men from a serious confrontation. If the
Cossacks had fought who knows how many more broken
heads and limbs there would have been. And this is the
fellow I'm attempting to investigate. He shook his head
at his own folly. I must lay the past to rest. "Clear the
streets," he finally ordered Mitka. "Tell our worthy
citizens that there's no more to see today. Post one man
outside and send the rest back to headquarters. You shall
stay here." Volkov indicated a position near the

88

doorway. "Keep folk out; the place is closed for the time being." Turning to one of the hovering waiters, he ordered, "Some mead if you can find an unbroken barrel. And food, if possible." He righted a bench near the large stove and sat down, motioning the starets to join him. "I came here originally for a bit of food and something to drink. Will you join me?"

"It will be a pleasure," answered the starets with a smile, and pulling up his long kaftan, he made himself comfortable.

89

CHAPTER SEVEN

Volkov noted with satisfaction that Mitka was standing to the side of the entrance, his arms crossed, his feet firmly planted, staring belligerently at the Cossacks, who far from returning his challenging stare were now either asleep or in a state of drunken bemusement. Leaving his bailiff to guard the door, he turned back to the starets who was motioning his own disciple to a bench nearby. Inhaling the strong scent of spilled mead and vodka, which added to his thirst, Volkov called out to the host who was still surveying the damage with a disgruntled expression, "Well, can we be accommodated as to food and drink?"

"Yes, if any is left," he grumbled.

"Surely you have stores in some secure place these fellows haven't reached?" asked Volkov as he nodded towards the Cossacks. And the starets repeated reassuringly that he would see to it that the damage and whatever food and drink had been wasted were paid in full.

"Ah, yes, that is all well and good but what about the custom? I've lost custom as well. My regulars fled the premises when your little lambs began heaving benches and stools."

"Yes, yes, that too. Total the damages and present me with the bill." Volkov looked surprised that the starets was able to dispense such largesse and he caught the magistrate's skeptical expression. "Sudar, folk have been most generous to me and given me more than I need for myself. Normally it would go to the poor. But today, if these, my friends, cannot meet the bill, I shall help them out. Eh, Koltso?" The tall burly Cossack nodded and tugged at his beard.

"You are our little father," he mumbled, then leaning back against the wall and covering his ample stomach with his hands fell into a state just short of actual sleep from which Volkov suspected he could quite easily be roused back into action. He turned back to the host and ordered him to worry about their food first, then do his reckoning.

While they waited to be served, Volkov said, "In as much as they're behaving now, I shall forgive your friends this as well," and he touched the wound on his forehead, dark now with clotted blood.

"Ah, Magistrate, so they did that as well. I'm sure they are sorry."

"Tell them the law in Moscow does not like to be the object of missiles and that this had better be the last time."

"Of course, of course." One of the Cossacks rose

abruptly, staggered over to the starets, embraced and kissed him, then swayed back to his own bench. "See, they are good fellows. I'm glad you are showing them mercy, Magistrate. They would not like to be locked up and would chafe at fetters. It is ambitious men they are too. It is hetmen they want to be, eh, my friends," he added, addressing his unruly flock.

A waiter ventured cautiously in among the now quiet Cossacks, straightening stools and benches, picking up wooden utensils that had been tossed on the floor as well as the heavy coats and fur hats they'd discarded. While Volkov and the starets looked on, he got a broom and attempted to sweep up the shards of broken pottery and spills of food. The starets saw the magistrate's frown. "I repeat, these are good men; you mustn't think ill of them." To Volkov's annoyance, the starets wagged a finger in his face. "Remember God favors the bold and these men are in Moscow because of their victory over Kuchum Khan and his horde."

"So you've said."

"It was Yermak's doing," called out Koltso, temporarily roused from his reverie. "There lived the Cossacks as free men, all the Don and the Terek and the Yaik Cossacks, and their hetman was Yermak, son of Timofei..."

"Yes, Yermak Timofeyevich. Outnumbered, vastly outnumbered, yet they defeated the enemy in every battle." The starets smiled indulgently at his Cossacks. "Brave hearts, all of them."

"Well, little father," called out Koltso, "it isn't swine's ears we want to be. Nor ploughman and sowers of buckwheat dawdling on stove ledges of an evening, but free men. All over the steppe and on every hillock, Magistrate, is where you can find us."

Volkov smiled at the man. He was beginning to appreciate Koltso. That one expresses himself with some eloquence he thought. Turning to the starets, he asked, "And are you from the same place as these, since you know them all so well?"

From under his heavy lidded eyes, the starets stared back at Volkov for some time before answering. "Not precisely no. They, most of them, are originally from the Volga; some were boatman." He leaned closer to Volkov. "It is no secret that they were accused of attacks on merchant barges journeying to and from Astrakhan and had to flee further north one step ahead of the law. There they entered the private armies of the Stroganovs and the rest is history. All is forgiven now." He examined the hands he'd placed on the table, finally replying. "As for me, why, I was born in a northern ostrog. Yes, in a frontier fort. My people worked on church land nearby." He closed his eyes, and perhaps in the silence that followed, contemplated that far-off place.

"Then you are far from home, Father."

"Yes, I was called by the Lord and, leaving my wife and children with my people, went on a mission to preach and heal. For such a call may not be denied." He examined Volkov's expression. "Magistrate, I can see skepticism writ in your face." Volkov smiled his narrow-eyed vulpine smile and the starets laughed. It was a surprisingly pleasant laugh. "It is true all the same. From my early youth I had this gift and a keen insight into the souls of men and the ability to influence them. I could finally no longer resist and went on my journey. Where

94

it will end, only God knows."

"Tell me more, Father, for I have never seen the wide world. This is all I know." Volkov's broad gesture was meant to signify Moscow.

"If it is your wish I shall tell you more of my history." Volkov noted that he seemed in no way reluctant to describe his past. Or said a perverse demon in Volkov's brain, it was perhaps an already well rehearsed story. "I first traveled to other frontier ostrogs, then to Perm, so I know well the lands under Stroganov sway. I preached to the men engaged in the salt industry, one of that powerful family's most profitable enterprises, and had some success with the plain folk there. Later I traveled to the trading center of Nizhni Novgorod and now I am here, where I must say, I have been made most welcome. What a fine city this is, Sergey Volkov. What wonders there are here as compared to my humble frontier community. And, if I may say so, you have the world in your backyard and needn't seek it elsewhere. Your stone churches, too, astonish me. We have only simple wooden structures but cunningly made for all that, and with, I should say, as much art and perhaps more faith than have gone into this city's ornate buildings."

The host interrupted the starets by finally presenting his reckoning and simultaneously a waiter began putting food and drink on their table. Volkov indicated that Mitka, still glowering in the doorway, should be given some as well. "I shall pay for this," said Volkov, pointing to what had been placed on the table. "Give some to your disciple as well." He smiled at the starets, this time more sincerely. "For you have done me a service. Surely more heads would have been broken had my men been forced to do battle. Your peacemaking was done quickly and quietly and I am grateful. I regret that I can only repay you and your man with poor Advent fare. But the festivities will begin shortly and then we shall all dine on more than soured cabbage and watery vegetable broth. Of course we do have vodka," and he lifted his cup to the starets.

"Yes, vodka, which raises up an old woman's legs and rubs open an old man's eyes." Both men laughed. Then for some moments no one said anything as they began to eat and drink.

"I thank you for the meal as does my Fedka," replied the starets, adding as he nodded in the direction of his disciple, "he goes everywhere with me. He looks after me." Then he turned his attention back to his food and again he made a hardy meal and drank deeply. Drinking sparingly himself, Volkov studied him as he ate. The man's black robe and kaftan were, if anything, more stained then when he'd last observed him at the Shuisky dinner.

"Hair just as greasy, fingernails still dirty," mused Volkov, "but his manner—, I do believe I'm warming to the fellow a bit."

"You are curious about me, eh, Magistrate? You don't quite trust me, yet you feel you should." The starets smiled slyly back at Volkov.

The prescience of the starets startled Volkov. "It's as if," he thought, "the fellow can read my mind." Aloud he said, "What you say is true, Father, after all you are a stranger here and I am a man of the law and bound to have a suspicious nature after dealing with deceiving fellows day in and day out."

"I can understand that. Nor am I offended. It is your duty to be vigilant." Kozlov continued to smile but his disciple scowled at Volkov. Animosity seemed to issue in waves from his unprepossessing figure and for the first time Volkov looked at him carefully. But just as abruptly he lost interest in the short, pudgy fellow and turned his attention back to the starets.

"Will you be in Moscow long?"

"Until my mission is accomplished or as much as your humble servant can do. God tells me when and where to go."

Volkov thought it rather presumptuous of the starets to declare he was in direct communication with the Lord but didn't point it out. "Then you will be here for the Christmas festivities which begin in a few days?" The man nodded. "And these fellows as well?"

"Yes, but then they must start back with reinforcements for their chief. Their numbers have been greatly reduced since the beginning of Yermak's campaign against the Khan. They are also bringing him much needed arms. And of course the blessing on their enterprise of our good father, the Tsar. Indeed, our Prince is sending a most cunningly made suit of armor as a gift for Yermak."

Koltso spoke up. "Hey, little father, you must come to our lodgings and help us to celebrate the birth of Christ. You must keep us out of mischief and give us your blessing."

"That I will surely do."

"He can come too," said Koltso, pointing to Volkov. "He's been a reasonable fellow."

"An excellent idea," declared the starets. "Yes, we shall give you a taste of our frontier hospitality. And bring your bailiff as well so he can learn what good men these fellows really are. We shall wipe that scowl from his face."

"I gladly accept your invitation," said Volkov, "and accept for my man, Mitka, as well." He laughed when he saw that Mitka had been bending his head further and further towards them in an effort to catch every word and after hearing that he'd been asked to the festivities as well, begin to grin from ear to ear.

The two men finished their food while the host continued to hover in the vicinity to see if the bills were really to be paid. Volkov took care of his share and from the pouch attached to his belt, the starets pulled out enough coins to pay for the damages just as he'd promised amid reassurances from Koltso that he and his men would see that he was reimbursed. A greatly mollified host ushered his guests out into the street, ordering someone to bring forward the horses of the magistrate and his bailiff.

In the street a crowd, though smaller than before, was still gathered in front of the kabak and when the men emerged, word was passed along that the starets was present. At once folk, looking like stuffed dolls, bundled up as they were against the cold, pressed forward to touch his garments. Several men and women fell to their knees and asked for his prayers. "My children, of course I will pray for you as you must yourselves pray to the good God." He touched one of the women lightly on her kerchiefed head, afterwards taking one of her work-roughened hands, red with the cold, in both of his. She looked up and he smiled at her. "Be at peace, my daughter." The woman heaved a grateful sigh. Volkov observed that several of the Cossacks, including Koltso, were standing in the doorway of the kabak nodding approval of their mentor's actions just as the starets turned his attention to one of the younger women. She was kneeling in the dirty snow of the street and he lay both hands on her shoulders. "My lovely child, do not be troubled," he said. As Volkov stood watching, he heard one of the Cossacks snigger.

"That one would make a good fuck." Volkov turned sharply and saw Koltso put a hand on his companion's arm and shush him. At his urging the Cossacks withdrew into the kabak. Volkov turned thoughtfully back to the starets just as he was making the sign of the cross over the young woman and blessing the rest of the crowd as well. He made as if to leave but men and women continued to surround him, making it difficult for him to move. Some of them ventured timidly to touch him on his sleeve. He was able to advance only a few paces, Volkov at his side. "Eh, Magistrate, we Rus are a religious folk, we have great faith, we are true believers." He didn't wait for any kind of reply but slowly passed through the crowd, his disciple following him.

Mitka and Volkov stood staring after him. "That is one good fellow," declared the bailiff.

"Yes, no doubt," replied Volkov, dismissing his incoherent doubts about the starets at least for the time being. He saw Mitka turn at stare back at the kabak.

"Those fellows should probably be in the lock-up until they're ready to go back where they came from,

Sudar."

"They're peaceful enough now. And I daresay we won't have any further trouble. If we do, it would probably be best if we sent for Father Yakov right away. He quieted them quickly enough." Volkov laughed. "And remember they are heroes, doers of great deeds. In honor of their victories, church bells were rung at the special request of the tsar." He frowned. "Moreover, they are still under his protection."

"Yes, yes I know all that. All the same I'll be glad to see the last of them." Mitka paused, remembering, "That is, after they've shown us that bit of hospitality they promised." He stopped, then after some thought, added, "I suppose this starets will leave one day too and go elsewhere to preach."

Volkov agreed, thinking privately that it couldn't be soon enough. "I'm weary of disturbing myself over this strange fellow."

Mitka removed his hat the better to scratch his head and as if that helped his ruminating, tentatively offered a possible connection between the Cossacks and the crimes that they needed to solve. "Sudar, you heard how they spoke of women. It was no way kindly or respectful, but rather quite coarse."

Volkov nodded, "A notion that should indeed be pursued. Look to it, Mitka, trace their comings and goings from where they are staying. Despite their supposed minders, if indeed, they've been assigned minders, see how they've managed to disrupt the peace and quiet of this neighborhood. And they'll surely want more than drink. Women must be available to them somehow. Or if not, just maybe at least one of them could be responsible for the rapes. Anyway, let me know what you find out."

CHAPTER EIGHT

"Smell the meat pies, Mitka, at last our fast is over." Volkov looked over the great market square in front of the Kremlin with approval even as his bailiff sniffed the air in order to take in all the delicious odors. "Purchase two of those pies," said Volkov, handing some coins to his man. As Mitka hurried toward the nearest food vendor, Volkov began slowly leading his horse past the merchants and shoppers, continuing to eye the scene with pleasure. Lanterns were being lit against the encroaching darkness and buyers and sellers alike were warming themselves at glowing braziers, defying the cold, determined to complete their business. Mitka presented him with a meat pie which he removed his mittens to eat. "A little something to tide us over until tonight's feast, eh?"

"Yes, roast goose is what my Lenochka is preparing, a fat juicy goose, Sudar, and blinis with cream, kutya, honey cakes, all the good things of the season," mumbled Mitka through a mouthful of crumbs. Volkov watched him close his eyes, perhaps the better to see the array of dishes he'd described. But Mitka's eyes popped open when an older lad suddenly jostled him A whole band of these boisterous youths, were laughing, shouting, and shoving aside the shoppers, some of whom had difficulty retaining their parcels.

"Ho, there, you imps of the devil," shouted Mitka, spraying crumbs every which way. "Stop running; you'll injure folks." The youths came to an abrupt standstill and looking at Mitka holding the horses' reins in one hand and a partly demolished and crumbling meat pie in the other, chortled long and loud. They made faces and stuck out their tongues.

One saucy fellow took a step forward and called out, "Hey, comrades, look at that fellow with the horse that looks like a bag of chaff. Thinks his own shit doesn't stink." He put up a hand and made a derisive gesture at the bailiff. Then the group, still shouting insults, ran down a narrow lane between houses. Spluttering, red-faced with anger, Mitka turned as if to mount his horse. Unable to resist a smile, Volkov reached out to restrain him.

"Let the rascals go. You'll not catch them in any case down the twists and turns of the lane they've chosen to go. I daresay you and your horse might do more damage to our citizens then those fellows and their elbows." Trying to mollify his man's indignation, he added, "There's bound to be mischief tonight and during the rest of the festivities. Everyone is excited after the restrictions of Advent. There'll be plenty of thumps exchanged as well, but it's not our business. Plenty of streltsy are in the square to keep order as well as to pounce on those a bit too careless with their fires." After a harumph or two, Mitka relaxed, finally finishing his pie in one great gulp.

Bells rang somewhere as Volkov finished his own pie and he wiped his greasy fingers on a great kerchief pulled from his sleeve. Continuing to amuse himself by looking around the square, he noted the jugglers and puppeteers around whom were gathered crowds of adults as well as children. And tumblers, their motley garb a complement to the fantastical domes and towers of the Church of the Intercession. "When everyone feels good," commented Volkov, "they're inclined to share with these poor itinerant fellows as well." He reached into the pouch attached to his belt. "Give them each some coins. I'm only sorry the children aren't here. How they'd laugh at the antics of Petrouchka. I must make the time to bring them here during the Christmas season."

"A raggle-taggle bunch but clever too. I like them myself, yes these skomorokhi, these minstrels, treated with kindness by our Prince himself, or so I've heard," said Mitka, counting out and adding a few dengi of his own. Coming back to where Volkov was waiting, he gestured towards the toy stalls. "Look, Sudar, it's those fucking Cossacks again. Are we to see them everywhere we look? And looking just like pigs at a new gate."

"Let them enjoy the wonders. At least they're behaving themselves now. Besides, Mitka, look behind them."

"Streltsy!"

"Yes, streltsy of their own. A permanent guard. A word to the palace that it would pay to keep them out of mischief. The guards can always remind our Cossacks that the tsar's favor can also be withdrawn."

"Good notion, Sudar. And I suppose you gave the palace the hint?" Volkov nodded. "But look at them now, interested in wooden toys, just like children." Mitka gave a derisive snort.

Volkov pulled his horse in that direction and Mitka followed. "I must get something for my two little chickens as well." Koltso recognized the magistrate and saluted before he and his comrades vanished elsewhere in the square, their streltsy custodians trailing behind.

In a few moments a merchant was showing Volkov his stock. "See, Magistrate, when the string is pulled the bear rears up in a most fiercesome manner. Oh, and this one sirs, see it is a cunningly carved little woodsman chopping with his axe." Mitka, all scorn earlier at the naivete of the Cossacks, was now playing with the toys himself, causing the merchant no little anxiety.

"See, Sudar, this one here. How clever!" Volkov laughed and purchased the rearing bear for his son and at another stand, a plump stuffed doll clad in a bright red sarafan and kerchief for his small daughter. The toys tucked into his saddlebags, Volkov was ready to remount when he heard someone calling.

"Sudar, Sudar, I'm glad I was able to find you." Volkov saw Luka on horseback making his way carefully through the crowd.

"From the expression on his face this is sure to be bad news," grumbled Volkov. "Yes, what is it?" he asked, then held up a hand. "Wait, the whole square needn't know." And he led his own mount to a more secluded spot.

Luka dismounted. Leaning close to his superior, he whispered, "Magistrate Pugachev sent word to our headquarters. He has apprehended his murderer. That is, he's seized the fellow that murdered the young woman in his district. And I believe the man's confessed."

"To our murders as well?"

"No, Sudar, but Magistrate Pugachev says you may come and question him if you wish. Now, if you desire. His bailiff is still there but Magistrate Pugachev will be gone. He has guests coming tonight.

"As have I. My wife's family is expected to dine with us."

"Oh, then there will be the devil to pay if you don't show up at home," Mitka blurted out, crossing himself instantly for protection against the evil one as well as apologizing for his indiscretion.

Volkov frowned at him but agreed, "You're right, there will be the devil to pay if I'm not there to support my wife. But this other matter is important as well." He shrugged, finally declaring, "It's not that late. Let's go and see this fellow and then we can go home." They made their way out of the square, leaving all the color and laughter behind and on less crowded thoroughfares rode to Pugachev's headquarters.

While Volkov was still in the process of dismounting, Mitka had already tossed his reins to a guard and gone in search of his bailiff acquaintance. When Maleev was found, both men hurried back to escort Volkov inside. "Where's this fellow?" Volkov demanded.

"In our lock-up."

"Who is he? And did he confess quickly? Or had you to resort to force?"

"As to who he is, why he was acquainted with the young woman that was murdered. He'd made a pest of himself around her or so her people say." The bailiff laughed. "As to confessing readily, why he did no such thing. Claimed he was innocent as they all do. Pretended great sorrow because the woman was dead. But he didn't fool us. This is one dog who knows whose meat he ate. He couldn't claim to be elsewhere; no one would vouch for the fellow. And many witnesses say the woman wanted no part of him, rejected him quite openly in fact." He stopped before adding in a sneering tone, "No doubt after first leading the fool on, eh? As everyone knows these daughters of Eve too often play the siren, eh? They look at us and laugh and shake their hair, making us their dupes, eh?" Each 'eh' was pronounced so emphatically, that Volkov felt he'd been jabbed with a finger. "They throw their kisses and say 'come to me' and we are lost." He lowered his voice. "Like rusalki, they lead us into mortal danger. And," he added, "this was no virgin like that youngster of yours."

To Volkov's surprise, Mitka kept bobbing his head in agreement. "And yet he has a good hard-working woman at home who's never strayed."

"Kuzmich may have killed her in a rage. He obviously bore her a grudge. Moreover the fellow's known for having a bit of temper. Indeed some say that the woman seemed to fear him. So we applied pressure. He confessed readily enough then. As to your victims, we questioned him briefly about them. Says he didn't do it. But it's for you to press that point, we didn't. I daresay Mitka could get the truth out of him soon enough. Never saw a fellow that acted guiltier. And as your man keeps telling me, the crimes are similar. Do you want to question him now?" Volkov hesitated. "He won't go away, Magistrate." Maleev laughed. "No, he'll be with us til he's hung, which will be a little while yet. Has to be reported higher up first, eh?"

Volkov thought of Sofya, his dinner, and his guests. "Yes, I'll put it off until another day. But soon, it must be soon. Perhaps tomorrow, or no, better the day after that. I have a commitment tomorrow as well," he added, remembering he'd been invited to the Shuisky home the following evening, an invitation not to be ignored.

Outside he dismissed Luka, allowing himself to be escorted home by Mitka. To him he commented, "I don't entirely trust confessions extracted by such methods. I will interview the fellow myself and we shall see." Mitka shook his head. Volkov's skepticism about the use of torture to extract information was something he'd never understood. It seemed perfectly reasonable to him. After all everyone knew how easy it was to lie.

During his journey home, Volkov mulled over what little information they had about the murders but at his gate he shook himself, thinking, "This isn't the time or the place for such dismal thoughts." He dismissed Mitka, calling after him, "Enjoy your fat, juicy goose and give my greetings to your good wife."

Remembering to remove the toys from his bags, he looked around the courtyard, and was chagrined to find that some of the guests had arrived before him. Sofya greeted him with a frown. "Serezhenka, finally," she said, and not waiting for a reply she ordered a servant to take his hat and coat. "Father and Mother have already arrived and my brothers and their wives are due shortly," she whispered in his ear. Leaving him to say his prayers and greet his in-laws, she turned her attention to the table, showing the maidservants where to place the food and ordering a manservant to pour mead for her parents. To still another maid she called out orders to keep the baby, Katya, out of mischief. Pavel, Volkov saw, was already sitting on his grandmother's lap. Before Volkov had a chance to sit down, he found himself back in the vestibule embracing and kissing the rest of his in-laws. Soon the hall was filled with laughter, noise, and the press of bodies. In one brief moment of quiet, Volkov regretted the loss of his own parents and one brother and then he shook off his feeling of dejection and sat down to exchange news with his father-in-law.

Food was served and mead drunk in copious quantities. The children, allowed some license for a change, shrieked with laughter. A servant opened the door into the hall and called out, "The singers have arrived. Volkov rose to welcome the band of singers and soon they were stamping the snow off their feet and jostling one another in their eagerness to enter the hall. The women and children cried out in mock fright as the masked figures darted forward, retreated, and darted forward again. "Look," cried Pavel, "that one is a horse and that one a goat." The figure masked as a goat brought the Cossacks to mind and Volkov silently reprimanded himself for allowing their crude behavior to intrude into the festivities.

"See, that is the Dead Man," shrieked one of the younger girls in mock terror. And the 'dead man' obligingly grinned at them all with long teeth made of turnips before collapsing on the floor and breathing his last while his companions pretended to sprinkle him with holy water and noisily bless him. The audience cheered and applauded. Then resurrected, he bowed, giving them another ghastly grin.

"A song, we must have a song," shouted Volkov over the din. And they began to sing.

"The spirit had come this festive time."

Ah, we walked and we searched for the spirit of Christmas

In all of the courtyards and all of the streets.

Finally through gates of gold and copper we found it in the Volkov yard.

We went up the stairs," the singers stamped their feet, "the door opened." They mimed a door opening and closing.

"The master, Sergey, is the shining moon." They bowed to Volkov.

"The mistress is the sun." Sofya received a bow as well. "Their children are the stars." Pavel and Katya clapped in delight.

"To the master and mistress we wish good health for all the many years," the singers shouted less than tunefully, afterwards pausing for breath. The audience applauded with great enthusiasm and the mummers bowed again.

"More, more," called out the company, "give us another song", and the singers obliged.

"The sausage is done
It sat in the stove
It looked at us
If the master gives us no pie," loudly chanted the
singers, thrusting their way to Volkov, "we'll seize
his mare by the tail.
So give us a sausage and a cake stuffed with suet
A tree-sized sausage and a plate-sized slice of pie
And we will bless you."
Sofya called the servants and they brought plates of
especially prepared cakes shaped like cows and lavishly
topped with sausages.
"Ah, a noble mistress, may your grain be heavy,
for you have given us pie.
We'll not pelt your windows nor your gates.
You'll only have our blessing."
They sang a further few songs then still eating
their booty, laughing, and pushing and shoving one
another playfully, they went out the door, off to the next
homestead with their Christmas songs and demands.
"My daughter has done us proud," said his father-
in-law and Volkov agreed. "The kitchen betrays the
house and I see and smell nothing but good things here.
Undoubtedly her mother taught her well." And he sent a
smile of approval to Sofya. Turning back to Volkov, he
asked, "No work for you surely from now until
Epiphany?"
"I'm afraid magistrates must always be available.
Crimes keep on being committed. Criminals don't let up
for the holidays."
"You poor fellow, but at least this evening you're
free to enjoy yourself and not think about the wickedness

out there." And the older man nodded in the direction of the door and the street beyond.

"Yes, I'm free to think of other things." As the father-in-law turned to speak to one of his sons, Volkov's thoughts turned to the murderer in his dank cell, his only company other felons. "No kvass and pies for him this Christmas Eve," he whispered. Sofya saw his frown and motioned him back to his duties as host.

One of her brothers approached Volkov. "I'm filled here," he said patting his stomach, "but not here," and he pointed to his head. It's time for a few old stories, don't you think. Father has brought our old Vanka for just that purpose. The fellow is filled with skazhi from head to toe. Isn't that so," old uncle?" he called out to an ancient who'd been quietly eating meat pie and soup near the stove. The old fellow gave them all a pleasant smile.

"Come and tell us tales when you've finished," Volkov invited.

"I am ready now, Master," he replied. And he rose with great dignity, brushed the crumbs from his long grey beard and held out his hands to the children. "What do the children wish to hear?" Favorite tales were shouted out to him.

"Sadko, please."

"No, no, Ilya Muromets and his battles with Nightingale the Brigand."

"Not that one, we just heard it," declared Pavel. "Do instead Dobrynia's fight with the dragon.

"Yes, yes, that one," they finally all agreed. And everyone settled back to hear the old tale, Volkov as well the others. He was more determined than ever to see to it that the family had a good Christmas Eve, complete with the traditional dishes, fortune telling and songs.

CHAPTER NINE

Shivering with cold and blinking at the glare of sunlight on the snow, Volkov grumbled, "A good day to remain next to one's stove, not one to go wandering about the city." But at least the prodigious feasting, on the part of those who could afford it as well as the drinking done by even those on the fringes of society, meant less traffic on the thoroughfares though that did not help his hungover condition. He thought of the generous feasts the last few evenings, first the ones at home, then yesterday at the home Ivan Andreyevich. How the vodka had foamed and sparkled and hissed last night. "So today I must pay for my overindulgence."

Nevertheless he continued to urge his mount forward and he and his bailiff were waved through the newly opened gate into the Skorodom district by the streltsy on duty. The two men dismounted in the courtyard of Pugachev's headquarters. Alerted by the noises, Maleev was on the stairs ready to greet them.

"Ah, Sudar, you and your man are welcome. However, Magistrate Pugachev will not be present today. He again has obligations at home and so unfortunately cannot be here to greet you." Volkov saw him exchange a wink with Mitka.

Either nursing his own hangover, sourly thought Volkov, or preparing for yet another feast. Aloud, he said, "We needn't bother him in this matter. I've come to interview that prisoner of yours. By the way, what is this fellow's full name?" he asked, at the same time ducking his head in order to enter the low doorway.

"Semyon Kuzmich, Sudar. And I shall fetch him here at once. The lock-up has several prisoners. You would have no privacy there. And conditions, well---." He shrugged eloquently and Volkov could well imagine the fetid atmosphere and depressing chill of the lock-up. "Meanwhile I shall have hot mead fetched for you at once." He winked at Mitka again, silently promising him some as well. Noting that Volkov winced at the suggestion of mead, Maleev added slyly, "If, of course, that is agreeable to you, Magistrate?" Gesturing his approval, Volkov tossed his mittens to Mitka. Then having been shown to an honored place near the stove, he opened his coat and removed his hat.

"I wish to be alone with the prisoner when he arrives. You two, go somewhere else on the premises." Mitka frowned. "The fellow will be shackled, so he's no danger to me and never fear, I will give you a summary of the exchange."

While he was waiting for the prisoner, Volkov sat with his eyes closed wishing the remaining ache in his head would go away. Sofya had done her best, mixing a concoction infallible for hangovers and it had done the trick up to a point, but he could still feel the nausea and throbbing hovering just there at the edge. A sip of the hot mead when it finally arrived slightly improved his condition and he sat back and relaxed. Almost nodding off in the warmth, he was suddenly pulled out of his pleasant stupor by Maleev's announcement that Semyon had arrived.

Volkov opened his eyes and saw a wretched bunched-up figure, shackled just as he'd predicted, prodded forward by Maleev. "I am not rising and don't wish to stare up at this fellow, so bring him a stool. Let him sit as well." Surprised, Maleev nevertheless did as he was bid. "Now, leave me alone with him." Maleev tugged at Mitka's sleeve because he seemed reluctant to go and finally both men left the room.

The prisoner grasped a blanket tightly around himself and lowered his head into it. Like a turtle in his shell thought Volkov. "Apparently trying to gain a bit of warmth or perhaps to hide himself inside its meager limits." Ordered to look up, the fellow reluctantly raised his head. Volkov was surprised. "I expected, though God knows why, some depraved wretch, evil written all over his countenance. I should have known," he mused, "I've seen enough brigands and murderers that looked perfectly harmless. But this one is just a boy. Innocent in appearance, diabolic in deed if his confession is true."

"How old are you, Semyon?"

"Eighteen, Gosudar," the boy mumbled, at last turning his beardless, freckled face completely in Volkov's direction.

"And a murderer already." The young man said

something in reply but so softly, Volkov couldn't hear him. "Speak up."

"Yes, I suppose so," he murmured.

"Either you are or you aren't, you young fool."

"I confessed I did it." His reply pierced the air, clear, sharp, and bitter.

"I want the history of your relations with this woman. And what are you by the way? How do you earn your bread?"

"I'm a carpenter's helper." Semyon lowered his head, again pulling the blanket higher as if seeking shelter in its folds but his movements made him grimace with pain. From the knout, surmised Volkov.

"Continue," he ordered.

"I knew the girl," replied the boy, sighing deeply. "Sveta was very pretty. Lively too. I am very sorry that she's dead."

"Did you have carnal relations with her?"

"What?" The lad stared at Volkov in confusion.

"Did you fuck her?" Semyon hung his head.

"Yes." His reply was the merest whisper.

"Did you force her?"

After a long pause, Kuzmich admitted as much. He seemed about to say more but stopped. Volkov motioned him to continue. "Afterwards she wanted none of me. Now God is punishing me."

"When did this rape take place?"

"Oh, months ago."

"And did you rape and then kill her a week ago?"

"I said I did, didn't I. I deserve my punishment." He turned his ashen, dirty face to Volkov for a moment, then looked down again.

"Were you in the Belgorod district and did you commit a similar crime there?"

"No," he replied, and seemed genuinely startled by the question. "What do I have to do in that district?" he asked in some confusion. "I travel only around my own neighborhood." His tone became more truculent. "You can beat me further but I will not confess to a second murder." Then the brief display of defiance disappeared and he hung his head again.

"Semyon, can you account for your time on the evening of the third of December and early on the morning of the fourth?"

The young man thought about it. He frowned and opened and closed his eyes with the effort. Yet the answer when it came was firmly stated. "Of course I can. I sleep in the same room as my master, the carpenter, and his family. No way to sneak off there."

"Yet the night of the murder here, you have no witnesses who can vouch for you at home."

"I stayed out late. For once I was determined to slip away from my tight-fisted master. I slept in the stable when I came back, so I wouldn't disturb the family. Used a horse blanket and slept in the hay. Not too bad a place even on a cold night. But the master missed me and drubbed me well for it the next day."

"You say you were out. Out where?"

"Out with a few friends for drinks."

"Yet I hear they are only willing to vouch for you in the early part of the evening."

"Drunk themselves is why. I closed the place with them."

Volkov shook his head. "According to your

friends you could have been out raping Sveta."

"And murdering her of course," the young man snarled in reply. Volkov found himself looking into a pair of vivid blue eyes, the whites shot with red from weeping or sleeplessness or both. "Ah, why torment me further, hang me and be done with it. With Sveta gone I don't want to live anyway. And if I suffer perhaps God can forgive me." He began to weep loudly, the sobs quite painfully wracking his slender hunched form.

What a dismal business, thought Volkov. He's a rapist for sure, but a murderer? Still he's confessed. But not yet to the murders in my district. I daresay we could beat another confession out of him if his master won't vouch for him. Before I draw any further conclusions, this carpenter and his family had better be questioned and I shall do that myself. Volkov loudly called for Mitka who must have been waiting with an ear to the door he arrived so quickly. A lot of good it's done him, for the thickness of the wood surely prevented him from hearing anything, and Volkov couldn't help smiling at his obviously frustrated bailiff. Aloud, he said, "Maleev can return his prisoner to the lock-up. Have our mounts readied and find out the location of the prisoner's master. We shall pay the fellow a visit."

When they were mounted, Mitka informed Volkov that he'd received the carpenter's address. "But it's some distance from here. And it will be past noon before we get there," he added in plaintive tones.

"No matter. That's our destination. Carpenters stay on their property, so presumably this fellow will be at home." Looking at his bailiff, who was attempting a pinched and hungry look belied by his sturdy, well-fed frame, he finally said, "Mitka, I promise you that after this interrogation, we shall go and find a good kabak near the Kremlin and make a hearty meal." Mitka began to grin.

"Sudar, you are getting just like the starets, you can tell what a fellow is thinking."

"A mixed blessing, if it is true," he replied softly to Mitka's retreating back for the bailiff was already thrusting his way forward clearing a path through the pedestrian traffic.

The carpenter wasn't so easily found because neither man was well-acquainted with this district of Moscow. Mitka repeatedly had to ask for directions. But at last he rode back to Volkov and announced, "We're near the place." He glanced around at the dwellings, some of them quite humble. "At least with the snow, this area looks almost presentable. Easier to travel as well what with the mud being frozen. I'm glad I live in the Belgorod, Sudar. Look, at the defenses, what paltry walls, nothing but dirt supported by planks. If the Tatars raid again like they did twelve years ago, I would prefer our own brick walls to these wooden palisades."

"Let's hope no such raid occurs again." Mitka nodded agreement and sent heavenward a long and fervent prayer.

"Here we are, Sudar. This, or so that last fellow said, is the home of Kabanov, master carpenter." The two men rode into the open courtyard and startled a woman carrying feed to her chickens. Still clutching the grain in her apron, she simultaneously attempted to bow and to retreat towards the stairs where she began shouting.

"Motka! Motka! Come quickly, the law is here."
A short stocky man not unlike the bailiff in appearance
opened the door and stepped out onto his porch a piece
of bread still clutched in his hand.

"Sudar, it seems we've disturbed the fellow's
meal." Mitka rode forward, and indicating Volkov with a
gesture, announced, "Here is my master, Magistrate
Volkov from the Belgorod district. Come to question
you about a serious crime."

The fellow's face had blanched at the first sight
of Volkov but he recovered quickly. He bowed and
nodded but there was an air of truculence about his
deference. "It's about that no good Semyon, I suppose.
What else could it be, for I am a law-abiding Christian."
As he was speaking, he further emphasized his identity
with the law abiding by punching himself several times
in the chest. "Sudar, I've already told Magistrate
Pugachev's men everything I know." Defiantly he
shoved the last of the bread into his mouth and chewed
in offended silence.

"We desire further information, uncle. And while
there is nothing to fear," said Volkov, "I do need to ask
some questions. And I do not wish to do it out here."
Grunting acquiescence, Kabanov motioned the two men
into the house. Mitka gave over the reins of their horses
to a curious neighborhood youngster who'd peeped into
the carpenter's workyard to see what was amiss.

Volkov looked around the main room of the
carpenter's home and saw that the other members of the
family were still seated around the table obviously
petrified by his visit. At a frenzied signal from Kabanov
they hastened to rise and bow. Volkov acknowledged

their bowing and scraping. He turned towards the icons and said a brief prayer and thought he heard a collective sigh of relief. Afterwards Kabanov indicated his two sons, a daughter, and still another apprentice, before announcing, "Me, Matvey Kabanov, I'm a God-fearing Christian so are all here present and we can answer your questions without fear. Woman," he bellowed to his wife, "fetch some kvass and bread for the masters." To Mitka's disappointment, Volkov refused but he did motion Kabanov back to his stool and sat down on a bench himself.

"Well, sirs, what do you wish. I am at your service." With a loud moan, Kabanov added, "That misbegotten Semyon has caused me nothing but trouble. Oh, the disgrace of it. Would that I had never taken him on."

"Motka, the boy wasn't so bad. I'll never believe he murdered anyone."

"What do you know about anything?" retorted Kabanov. Still clutching her apron load of grain, his wife sat down looking mulish but she kept silent.

Volkov went on to describe the murders that had been committed in his own district and explained that the murders in both districts appeared to have been done by the same man. "There were important similarities. So I am asking if your man's time can be accounted for on the date in question."

"Our Semyon was here that night as he was every single night except when that trollop, Sveta, was strangled. She led the boy on, I say. It is known that he pursued her but---." This outburst came from Kabanov's wife and she stared at her husband defiantly as she attempted to continue.

"Hold your tongue, woman," he commanded. Glaring at her, he made a fist. She clamped her lips together and he turned back to Volkov. "I have to agree. What my old woman says is true. The boy was not allowed out to carouse though he whined and complained that I was too severe. Hah, if he'd obeyed me, he wouldn't be in the lock-up now. Besides if he stumbled in drunk what kind of work would I get from him the next day? But when Sveta was murdered, yes, he was out all night. I found the rascal in the hay the next day sleeping it off. He got a sound beating for it too. Little did I know that he was up to worse than getting drunk." Volkov saw the woman shake her head in denial. "But, Sudar, no other day did he escape my vigilant eye." He looked around at the others in the room. "An eye like a falcon that is what I have." And he pointed to his eye to make sure that Volkov understood. His sons looked as if they unhappily agreed. "And how could Semyon get to your district anyway? He wouldn't have dared to use my old nag. Indeed, where could the lad stay? He knows no one there. No, the night you've mentioned, the rascal was right here in this room snoring away as usual. Isn't that so," he asked the others and they all nodded in agreement. "I will take an oath on the cross for you that this is all true. We will all take oaths on the cross for you," he declared in righteous, ringing tones. "No, Magistrate, you will have to look elsewhere for your murderer. It wasn't Kuzmich, that's for sure." He struck the table with a powerful fist. "If only I'd gone looking for him that evening when I saw he'd slipped away. Sveta! My woman's right there. Her people didn't keep a tight rein on the girl. She led him on and it's no wonder she came to a bad end." He stopped talking and waited for a response.

Volkov rose. "I'm satisfied you are being truthful. We will have to find our villain elsewhere." Kabanov nodded and led the way back to the yard. Mitka tossed a coin to the lad holding the reins and retrieved the horses. The two man mounted and rode back to the heart of the city.

"Nothing for us here, eh, Gosudar?"

"No there isn't."

"Perhaps a bite to eat then," hinted Mitka.

"Yes, we'll quiet your worm." They rode back through the area of the Skorodom where most of the streltsy had their houses, eventually reentering their own walled district and then headed directly for the great market square in the Kitaigorod.

Two drunks lay in the snow drifts near the kabak Volkov had chosen for their meal and he notified the host who shrugged indifferently as if to indicate it wasn't his responsibility. Volkov's baleful glare made him change his mind and he ordered one of his waiters to drag the fellows into the stable with the hay and horses. "That should do for them," he announced to the magistrate. Satisfied, Volkov entered the kabak.

After sitting down in the room reserved for better clientele, Volkov ordered enough for the two of them. Mitka looked around the room and at the dishes quickly being heaped upon their table. "Sudar, I'm glad you chose this particular establishment. The cook is liberal with the garlic." Turning philosophic, he added, with a finger tapping his temple, "As the wise man knows, vodka, garlic, and a good steam bath regularly taken are what keeps a fellow in good health."

"I agree," said Volkov, laughing, but his expression grew more sober as he went on to describe in brief his interview with Semyon. An instinctive feeling that as far as he was concerned all the murders were still unsolved he kept to himself. After they both had their fill, Mitka left to get their horses. When Volkov stepped outside he blinked in the sudden bright sunlight, yet he felt cheered somehow by the sun's presence. "Let's wander a bit," he said to Mitka, when the bailiff returned with their mounts. "It's warmer now and the sunlight makes everything sparkle. Let's enjoy the sun which is after all most valued when it is furthest away."

Mitka nodded. "And see, Sudar, the colors, they are so bright against the snow." He indicated a crowd which had gathered near the porch of Ivan's fantastical church and was presenting a vivid canvas of reds, yellows, and blues. When they approached that end of the square, Volkov saw what was undoubtedly a yurodivyi. Mitka hung back but Volkov, curious to see the holy fool and his antics, motioned him forward.

Scantily clad in spite of the low temperature, thin to the point of emaciation, unkempt, and presenting a dark spot among the colors of those who surrounded him, the man was in addition festooned with chains. He rattled these periodically at the onlookers who remained respectful even as they laughed at some of his foolish antics. The man was elderly and Volkov marveled at the vigor he was able to display. He darted up to the stalls of the merchants and touched their goods with his dirty fingers all the while shaking his head from side to side.

One merchant rapped him across the knuckles with a
small rod. The old man smiled and blew on his abused
fingers. "I thank him," he told the crowd. "Yes, yes, to
suffer is good." He waggled his fingers at the crowd and
ridiculing the vendors, cried out, "Tawdry goods.
Tawdry goods. Who'll buy my tawdry goods. They are
all that is worthwhile in my life." He hopped a bit and
the crowd laughed, even the overzealous merchant. "Yes,
yes I must protect my goods. Yes, need lots of goods to
get to heaven. Must have scarves and coats and boots."
He kicked the air with a foot wrapped in strips of cloth.
Another vendor offered him some food but he struck it
down with his hand and it crumbled on the ground. "Yes,
food, need lots of food to get to heaven."

"Ah, Mischa, you must eat," cried one old
woman.

A man, well-dressed and substantial, standing
next to Volkov leaned closer and whispered, "That is our
Mischa. He comes here often to hector us into better
behavior. He is a true one. Only one chosen by God
could withstand such hardships." And he looked at the
old man with reverential awe. Volkov nodded
agreement. They were both shivering a bit from the cold
and forced to stamp their booted feet now and then to
keep warm. Yet, Mischa, barely clad, didn't seem
affected by the cold at all.

"The rich are all destined for heaven," said the
holy fool, continuing his comments to the crowd. "The
poor, why them Saint Peter won't let in the door, eh?"

The holy fool stared at the men and women
around him with wild eyes and many ceased to laugh and
began to look around with an embarrassed air. "It is wise

what he is hinting," someone called out.

"The poor are rich; the rich are poor, eh?" Then he suddenly rattled his chains and darted in and out among them wagging a finger at this one and that one. "A little red rooster, he runs along the perch. He will run after you and you and you."

"What can he mean?" cried a woman, a worried expression on her face.

"What can he mean? What can he mean?" parroted Mischa.

"It is fire. He is talking about fire," called out someone else. With a groan he added, "He is predicting everlasting fire for us." Folk in the crowd began to cross themselves.

"How can we be saved, holy one?"

The old man tittered. "Soon you will all have patrimonial estates seven feet long." He let out an exaggerated and comical sigh. "But few are keen on the place." A few folk still laughed at Mischa's capers but most of the crowd appeared sober.

"Ah, ah," shrieked an old woman, "the holy one is talking about the grave."

Volkov noticed that the crowd wouldn't leave in spite of the fact that many were now more frightened than amused but continued to surge backward and forward following the holy fool's paces. He also remained with the crowd at the same time trying to shake off vague feelings of guilt about this and that. The man's wild eyes searched the crowd again, passing over Volkov who breathed a sigh of relief and lit instead on the figure of the starets who had just entered the square surrounded by his usual worshipful entourage. The holy fool darted up to Father Jakov and rattled the chains in his face.

"Who are you my son, a man or a devil? A man or a devil?" Volkov was close enough and saw the starets draw back. Yet because of the press of bodies, he couldn't retreat very far so instead he held up his hands in front of himself as if for protection. Volkov realized that the man was actually showing fear and he took a certain amount of satisfaction in his discomfort. "Perhaps the holy fool thinks as I do, that this fellow is not what he seems."

The old man put his head to one side and with a benign expression on his face, asked again in a mild voice, "Who are you a man or a devil?"

Fedka rushed towards the old man shouting but the starets called him back, grasping him firmly by the arm in order to restrain him. The folk around the starets at first startled by the accusations, started to hurl insults back at the holy fool. "Not right in the head," called out one of father Jakov's followers, pointing to his own temple and rotating his finger.

"Yes," said another, "he who has no wits can't lose them."

The followers of the starets laughed at these sallies, while those who had been listening to the holy fool, cried, "Shame! Shame!"

And still waggling a hand at the starets, the old man added, "One step taken to hell, puts you half way there, doesn't it?"

"He should be locked up," cried Fedka. "He dares to cast doubt on a truly good man," with gestures egging on those surrounding the starets. They began to advance ominously on the holy fool which roused his own supporters, the men and women to whom he'd been speaking in the square. Some of these began to throw imprecations at the starets and those around him.

"This one suffers for Christ. See his nakedness. See his chains."

"Our Mischa is a true one."

"Blessed are they who suffer for righteousness sake," shouted a stout young woman at the starets and waggled her market basket at him as well. Fearing it would come to blows, Volkov moved to intervene but before he could do so, the starets fell to his knees before the holy fool. "Beat me with your chains, scourge me with your imprecations for it is true that I am a sinner." Mischa smiled at the starets and lifted his hand, to beat or bless no one could tell, because suddenly Fedka intervened.

Seizing the old man by the arms, he shouted, "No, no, you shall not touch my master." The opposing forces in the crowd became still more vociferous and fists were raised. This time Volkov thrust his way between the opposing groups followed by Mitka who was generously applying his fists, first against one side then against the other, shouting the magistrate's name and rank all the while. They forced their way to the side of the starets. Volkov ordered him to rise and follow him out of the square. He rose though slowly and the situation calmed down. Deprived of the starets, the holy fool turned his attention elsewhere. The crowd either followed old Mischa or stood about in small groups discussing everything that had happened. Volkov, meanwhile, led the way back to the shelter of the kabak where he and Mitka had just eaten.

"Ah, Magistrate, this time you've prevented a crisis."

"I cannot understand why the holy fool should select you in particular for his strange comments."

"What can I say, Magistrate, except that we are all sinners and deserve to be reminded of it. Yes, I too admit as much." The starets lowered his head and tightly grasping the large wooden cross he always wore with one mittened hand, he continued, "I daresay only such a one is truly sinless for he has renounced the world and suffers most grievously for all our sins. Does not Saint Paul say, that to shame the wise, God has chosen what the world regards as fools?" Again the man surprised Volkov. He'd expected the starets to rant against his rival but now he seemed humble in the face of the holy fool's cryptic comments. He was angry at himself for constantly misjudging the man.

"Remember our evening engagement with the Cossacks in two days time, Magistrate. It will be at the house hired for Koltso and his men by the state. It is located in the Kitaigorod near the Church of Saint Nicolas. Ask anyone near there," he said with a smile, "they all know where the Cossacks are housed. And bring your man as well." The starets moved off slowly, his followers close behind, while Volkov looked on bemused by the whole episode.

"A strange episode, Gosudar," said Mitka, shaking his head as if still puzzled and Volkov nodded. "The holy man wasn't so bad nor so foolish, was he? I expected hell-fire and demons and that I didn't want to hear. One gets quite enough of such warnings as it is.

Still the old fellow made me uneasy. What the people thought he said, was it true do you think?"

"Some of it yes. But such men talk in riddles and I suppose we see the answers each according to our deserts."

"And that remark is somewhat perplexing as well," said Mitka scratching his head.

CHAPTER TEN

Hands on her hips, head cocked to one side, Sofya stood surveying her husband's appearance. "So you're off to these Cossacks. Will you stay the night, Serezhenka?"

"I do not have that intention now, but who knows what will happen?" replied Volkov as he was being helped into his coat by one of the servants.

"They are rowdy men I hear." She shook her head as if doubtful about the excursion. "Rough company."

"I shall be careful. Anyway, your Otyets Yakov will be there to protect me."

"Why do you persist in saying say that? He is not my Father Yakov," she declared, an exasperated expression on her face. "I only saw him the one time. Of course it still seems to me that he is a good man despite whatever suspicions you have about him. And," she added, wagging a finger at Volkov, "since that time I have heard nothing ill of him from any of the boyars' wives. They continue to speak well of him. So yes, I'm glad he will be there. He is sure to make the Cossacks behave themselves."

"So you think I can't take care of myself."

Sofya laughed. "It was you who mentioned him as protection. As to that, of course, I believe you can take care of yourself, yet in such wicked company you may be led astray and it is good that a holy man will be present to restrain the company." She stood back to look at him. "You are finely turned out at any rate. You shall be the handsomest man there." By way of thanks for the compliment, Volkov walked over to his wife and kissed her soundly.

"Don't worry about me; I shall be safe."

"Don't drink too much, Serezhenka."

"Don't nag. I plan to be careful. Besides, Mitka will be there for surety."

"Ah, you always make such promises and as for Mitka, why, he does what you do."

"We won't misbehave." As if on cue, a loud knocking at the door announced Mitka's arrival. Waving a brief farewell to his wife, Volkov turned and left.

"Already pitch dark and overcast, ah, Sudar, we need our lanterns this evening. No moon, no stars to see by. And I feel snow in the air." Accompanied by the bailiff's continuing comments, the magistrate and his escort made their way into the Kitaigorod. Torches held aloft, the guards at the barriers quickly passed them through. "And see there," said Mitka, pointing to two streltsy guarding the entrance to a small but substantial dwelling, "we've arrived and it seems the palace is taking no chances with these Cossacks. There are even guards here. Perhaps if you hadn't warned those in charge, the city might have come to believe that the Tatars had returned to raid."

"I'm sure others went to the palace with similar charges. Anyway, you shouldn't speak so disparagingly of your hosts. Haven't they given us a generous invitation to join them in their revels?"

Mitka agreed, but added grudgingly, "Ah, that is probably because they must be forever partying and need to look at faces other than their own." Volkov laughed first at his chief lieutenant's sour expression then at the way his face lit up. "Still, it will undoubtedly be a fine feast for it is the tsar himself who is providing for them. The food has surely been sent from the palace."

One of the streltsy recognized Volkov, saluted smartly and began ordering servants to see to the horses. "Your men are welcome to stay with us, Gosudar," he announced, and motioned the rest of Volkov's guard into the courtyard.

Mitka nodded his approval at the martial figure of the strelets, who'd re-shouldered his arquebus with one mittened hand and returned to his post. "They look smartly turned out and very fierce with their sabers and bullet pouches and their poleaxes but have they ever smelled even a bit of powder in a battle?" Leaning over, he attempted to whisper, "These fellows are only used to separating warring old besoms or fat belligerent merchants and putting out fires. I daresay the Cossacks could outfight them, weapons and all, for what do these fellows know about real fighting?"

"As much as you," thought Volkov unkindly as the two men stood dismounted inside the courtyard and watched both their men and their horses being led away.

Koltso was already watching from the stairs. "Welcome, welcome, Gosudar. I knew you had come. At the first sound of arrival, Otyets Jakov said to me, 'Why, Vanka, it is our Magistrate and his lieutenant come to join us'. Is that not remarkable, that he could announce the coming of strangers to our house?"

Mitka, who'd come to adopt Volkov's skeptical view of the starets snorted and whispered, "Hardly strangers, eh, Gosudar, more like someone who was expected any moment. What a simple fellow that Koltso is."

"Shh, it won't do to douse the light of the starets in the eyes of his good friends."

At the door, Volkov found himself embraced by Koltso and soundly kissed on both cheeks. "It's like being greeted by a bear. And something of a liberty as well, but I shall let it pass," he said to himself. Shown into the hall, he was greeted by cheers and raised cups. The Cossacks were sitting on benches around a long table. It was obvious they'd already begun their drinking but at least they were still upright and for the most part wide awake. The temperature of the room was such that Volkov was glad to hand over coat, hat, and mittens to an attendant. Even the lighter kaftan underneath my street coat will probably be too warm, he thought, as he eyed the Cossacks who were already stripped to their shirt sleeves.

"Ah, look, at your colors, Sudar! Such fine feathers!"

"Not such fine feathers. Most at the court would shake their heads at the plainness of my garb," he said discounting his appearance.

"Well, finer for us than what you see." Koltso pretended to count. "Two shiteaters, seven shitasses and two fuckers. Of course I'm not counting our good Otyets Jakov." The starets shook his head at his friend but Volkov was laughing loudly and promptly felt a bear paw on his back. "You are one good fellow, Magistrate."

The starets was sitting at the far end of the table looking enigmatic and unperturbed in so far as Volkov could see in the dim light made by the few candles and rushlights placed here and there around the room. Fedka, his usual belligerent expression firmly in place, sat at the side of his master.

"I wonder, Sudar," whispered Mitka, "does the good Father get to shit alone or does that fellow follow him there as well?" Again Volkov laughed out loud and Koltso assumed it was because he was happy to be there and said as much. He kicked the Cossack seated near the door.

"Hey, Petrukha, offer the Magistrate bread and salt. We must show we know how to be proper hosts." The Cossack in question rose and offered the bread and salt. Volkov thanked the company and they all cheered again, stamping their booted feet, creating enough noise, thought Volkov, to wake the dead. Koltso led the way to a seat near the starets who nodded a greeting. "A place of honor near our beloved Otyets. You, Fedka, make room for his man." Neither Mitka nor Fedka seemed pleased to be in proximity to one another noted Volkov as he seated himself, with the starets on his right and Koltso, rather too close, on his left.

"A drink," the burly Cossack shouted, and an attendant scurried to pour mead into Volkov's cup. "We've already begun and you must catch us up. Food too," he called, pounding a meaty fist on the table. He pushed a fresh steaming platter of meat pies towards the Magistrate. "A little cup and a little loaf, eh? It's good, you'll lick your fingers," the truth of which he proceeded to demonstrate by licking his own. Both Volkov and Mitka were soon well-served with food. Volkov looked at the mounds of food and was grateful that the Advent fast was over.

"We have music too. Hired some gusli players." He winked playfully at Volkov. "Perhaps later another surprise at well." Suddenly his expression sobered. "Let us all rise and drink to our gracious father, the Tsar. It is because of his generosity that we drink and dine so well tonight. It is he who has given us this overflowing sea." And he nodded towards the beakers, the flagons, and the ewers covering the table. So with a clatter as well as accompanying thuds and thumps, the entire company stood and drank deeply to the Tsar's health.

"Look at this, Magistrate," said Koltso after they were all seated once again, "thanks to the tsar the finest rye flour was used in this bread. Not something us poor fellows are used too. Coarse loaves, cabbage soup, and gruel that's our usual fare." He took an enormous bite of bread, then through broad gestures because his mouth was full, Koltso urged pancakes, fritters, and soup on Volkov. "Pelmeni too," he urged, finally finding his voice.

Rather than grudgingly, Volkov willingly dug

into the food and for some moments no one said much of anything. He also noted that Father Yakov was doing the same and wondered from whom he received his absolution. Then from the other end of the table, someone loudly called for riddles. "If we're to have no music yet, Vanka," the voice pleaded, at least let's play at riddles."

"What are you thinking of, Petrukha? The magistrate here will be thinking we are nothing but children instead of fierce warriors if we play such childish games. A peasant's game, eh?" Koltso asked, turning to Volkov.

"Not at all. I like a good puzzle as well as anyone. In Moscow such games are played too."

"Well, then we shall have a few riddles along with our food and drink. But, Otyets," declared Koltso, leaning across Volkov and addressing the starets, "you cannot play for you can see all the answers beforehand. It wouldn't be fair." Father Yakov neither denied or agreed with this declaration, he merely smiled and bade them get on with their game.

"You begin, Sudar. Give us a good one." Volkov smiled and sitting in silence for some moments attempted to recall an especially good riddle.

"Try this: Two sisters: One is fair, the other dark."

Putting all his energies into thought, Koltso frowned. "That is a hard one, Sudar. Comrades," he said, turning to the table at large, "you must help me."

Scratching a shaggy head of hair, Petrukha offered, "Is it perhaps really two sisters and the one is dark and the other fair?"

"No, you simpleton," shouted Koltso, "in riddles things are never what they seem on the surface. It has to be something else, but what?" Volkov sat back and sipped his mead. While the rest of the company tossed guesses back and forth, he studied the starets who was unusually quiet. "After breaking bread together at the kabak, surely we are well-acquainted and should be able speak easily," he thought. "Or perhaps he is still embarrassed because I witnessed that episode with the holy fool the other day. "

As if he knew what Volkov was thinking, the starets turned his gaze upon the magistrate. Again Volkov felt trapped by the man's large and luminous eyes. "One's eyes", he thought, "are supposed to mirror the soul, but I can't read anything in his." Without a word, the two men continued to scrutinize one another, neither willing to break contact, until finally Mitka, leaning across the table reminded Volkov of the game.

"Gosudar, perhaps they have an answer." In relief Volkov turned his attention back to the table at large.

"Is it day and night?" called out one of the men.

"Yes, it is. Very good." The men sitting near the fellow who had guessed correctly congratulated him with a toast.

"Another riddle," said Koltso. "Yes, another one and Otyets, you must give it to us."

"Certainly," he replied without a moment's hesitation. "It is this-I whirl, I growl, I care for no one."

"Comrades, another challenge," declared Koltso, grinning through his black beard. "We must all think hard." But the numerous guesses were all rejected by the starets.

"A Tatar?"

The starets smiled. "It fits, my son. But it is not the answer this time."

Finally they conceded defeat, pleading, "Give us a clue please, Otyets."

"Look out the door." Petrukha went to the door, opened it and peered out. "It's begun to snow," he announced coining back into the room.

"Hah, a snowstorm," shouted Koltso.

"You have it, friend," replied the starets. "A good night to be in a nice bright corner next to our own dear mother the stove and away from the icy fingers of Moroz."

"Yes, away from the frost demon. But, Otyets," asked Koltso, "how did you know it was snowing?" Then he hit his forehead with a balled fist. "Of course you knew. How deep this man is," he proclaimed to the company."

"And how wise." In tones of awe other compliments to Father Yakov's second sight were passed around the table.

Riddles continued to amuse the others but Koltso began relating his experiences in Sibir to his neighbors at the table. Genuinely interested in hearing about them, Volkov urged him on as did the starets. So Koltso described the hordes of Tatars that he and his men had faced. He paused during the narrative to toss a handful of salted pumpkin seeds into his mouth and how he ground them to mash was fearsome to behold. As if he were crushing Tatars, thought Volkov. Then with a finger Koltso picked between his teeth seeking the odd bit here and there before continuing.

"And the Khan, that dog of a Tatar, that spoiler,
why he knew the terrain. For us it was all new and
difficult. And there were so many of them and so few of
us. But our Yermak, he wasn't afraid. He said one of us
was worthy of ten, even twenty of them and so it proved.
No," he boasted, "I didn't shake in my boots until I came
here to Moscow. It was our Prince, you see. We knew
we'd angered him because our invasion unleashed
retaliatory raids into the territory of the Rus. And the
governors, oh how those fellows complained to our
Father, the tsar. And as everyone knows the Tsar's wrath
can be a messenger of death. But our Otyets, here, why
he came to visit us and spoke reassuringly. He told us the
fortune in furs we'd captured from old Kuchum Khan
and the victorious tales we'd tell would win him over. So
we went to the palace and braved the anger of our
Prince. And it was as you predicted, Otyets, the Tsar's
eyes blazed with fire but when I dared to speak and we
presented the furs, why then---. Then, Magistrate, those
same eyes gleamed with pleasure and he deigned to hear
our whole story. He ordered the bells to be rung in our
honor. Imagine that. Peals sounding throughout the city
for us poor fellows from the Volga. May our good
fortune continue." Koltso spat over his left shoulder as
insurance. "Justice is the Tsar's crown and wisdom his
scepter," declared Koltso, and Volkov was surprised to
see tears on his cheeks. His big paw reached around and
he embraced Volkov. With one arm still around the
Magistrate, he used the other to pound the table. "Let's
have the gusli players." And an attendant ran to fetch
them.

Removing his arm Koltso turned his attention to

the Cossack on his other side. Volkov leaned towards the starets, and said by way of conversation, nodding towards the burly Cossack leader, "I believe that he has reached the recommended three cups for the Orthodox."

"Oh, rather more than that, but not yet the God-offending, angel-rejecting, demon-rejoicing seventh cup." And the starets raised his cup and drank deeply himself. A smile played around his lips. "Come, Magistrate, even monks take one and I am after all only a poor muzhik myself and to us even bad kvass is better than water." He passed his hand over his cup of mead as if he were conjuring. "Is it not said of intoxication that it speaks to every man, to rich and poor alike, to beggars and princes, to young and old. Then our arms can hold the whole world and our head is high; our mind is equal to none. And though perhaps a mite disorderly, our tongue is eloquent and our eyes shameless."

Volkov looked at the starets with some surprise. Father Yakov waggled a long thin finger at him. "The holy fathers did not forbid us to drink though it is true they rejected drunkenness. But not to drink at all is an insult to the creation made by God. Drinking is a joy for the wise."

"And for those who are not so wise?"

"Ah, then it is a sin." Volkov wondered for a bit how one could draw the line then he laughed and held out his own cup for more.

Koltso noted the request and nodding encouragingly, placed another meat pie on the magistrate's platter, at the same time loosening his own belt and giving out a resounding belch. He waved his hand in the direction of the musicians. "Continue,

continue," he called to them.

One of the gusli players rose and announced a song in honor of Yermak which led to a general cheer. The Cossacks sat completely engrossed until the end of the song, then rose, cheered, stamped their feet, and threw coins to the player. "What a fine fellow," Koltso exclaimed.

"A clever one too. He knows his audience," said Volkov, leaning towards the starets, who promptly called out.

"Another riddle for you, my friends. It grew up in the forest. It was taken from the forest and when it's held it cries."

"Ho, ho, that is an easy one. It is a gusli of course," cried out several of the Cossacks at once.

The starets smiled benignly at the company. "You are too clever for me."

Koltso called for more music. "We shall sing as well. A song of our Mother Volga." He turned to the Magistrate with a touch of defiance in his expression. "Yes, that was our home and some called us brigands." He dismissed the accusation with a wave of his hand. "You there, musicians, do you know this tune?" And he began to hum a melody. They nodded and struck up the song. Koltso, who had a fine, deep voice, sang along with the players.

"Do not rustle, mother green oak,

Do not keep this fine young man from thinking about things!

For tomorrow they will take me to be questioned,

Before that terrible judge, the Tsar And the Gosudar-Tsar himself, he will ask,

"Tell me, tell me, peasant's son,
What have you stolen, what have you robbed,
Were there many comrades with you?"
"I will tell, Orthodox Tsar,
The whole truth will I tell,
There were four comrades with me;
The first was the dark night;
The second my knife;
The third my good horse;
And the fourth my taut bow;
My messengers were red-hot arrows."
And the Orthodox Tsar replied:
"Glory to you peasant's son.
That you knew how to steal,
Knew how to answer!
For this will I reward you
With a tall mansion in the midst of a field,
With two pillars and a crossbeam."

Koltso stopped after a long drawn out note and the musicians gave a final flourish. Some of the Cossacks wiped away tears. Koltso looked at the Magistrate. "Yes, brigands we were, but free men, nursed and fed by the Mother Volga. Then we fought for our Otyets, the Orthodox Tsar. And see he has rewarded us." He turned back to his men to receive their cries of approval.

Volkov nodded. "These are a different breed of men, a law unto themselves." He thought he rather admired their determination to be free of any restraints. He was hemmed in by restraints on every side. They feared no one really, perhaps not even the Tsar, while he had to act circumspectly at all times and feared recriminations from this official and that official. He found himself for a moment envying them.

"So, Magistrate," began the starets, startling Volkov out of this thoughts, "you see, these have committed grievous sins yet they have good hearts and are forgiven their transgressions by the Tsar himself."

"One must be sorry for one's misdeeds to be truly forgiven, is that not true?"

"Yes, it is true."

"And that is for God to decide. The state is another matter; it must punish."

"Vengeance is mine sayeth the Lord."

"We must keep order."

"The Tsar himself has absolved these men and will not punish them."

"Ah, yes, our Orthodox Tsar." There was a certain bitterness in Volkov's voice which the starets noted. He nodded sympathetically.

"You know yourself, Magistrate, if I read you correctly, how we Rus suffer grievously from the day of our birth. Surely this must soften your judgment towards our sins."

Volkov thought quietly for awhile. "I suppose, Otyets, it depends on what those sins are." They stared at one another until Koltso interrupted.

He winked at Volkov. "Now we have another surprise." He clapped his hands as a signal to one of the servants who opened another door and motioned a number of women into the hall. "Dancers, Magistrate, here in the city to earn their bread during the festivities." The dancers were past their youth but handsome nonetheless. They were made up even more heavily,

Volkov noted, than Muscovite women of the upper classes. Arms and ankles covered in bangles, heavy earrings dangling from their ears, the women rang like small bells as they walked around the table flaunting their charms. Dusky and dark-haired, they smelled of strange far-away places and were very appealing in their gaudy colors. Flinging their arms about, stamping their bare feet, they whirled in a wild abandoned dance with the Cossacks cheering them on. The music grew wilder, their skirts flew up exposing their legs and private parts. Volkov felt a shortness of breath and at the same time a sudden burgeoning between his legs. He looked at the starets and saw him taking in the scene as avidly as the other men, indeed as he was himself.

The starets caught the look and held out his hand in an odd supplicating gesture. "Even a saint," he murmured, turning his back to the women, "will turn his head when a naked whore is on display."

Koltso laughed in Volkov's ear. "Yes, that is true. There's an old song." He grinned, "Yes, another old song. I shall recite it." He leaned closer. "It was in the city of Kazan. A young monk was shorn. The monk felt like taking a walk. Beyond the holy gates. Beyond the gates was a park. In the park were some pretty maids. Well now, the monk looked. He threw up his cowl. "'Oh, burn, my boring cell. Vanish, my black garment. I, a young man, have had enough of being saved. Isn't it time for me to find a sweet, pretty maid?'" He roared with laughter at his own humor and the others joined him.

Only Fedka, Volkov noted, continued to frown but that was habitual with him. Making an effort to shake off his own alcoholic haze, he saw Fedka tug at his master's sleeve.

"Master, it is best if we left now. These women are not even Christian, Otyets. It is wrong to continue here. This lewdness is not for you," and he looked in alarm in the direction of the dancers who were bending to embrace the enthusiastic Cossacks. "Let us return to our lodgings."

Noting the coupling that was being to take place, the starets commented with something like a sigh, "A woman's desire is like a beggar's sack; it can never be filled." Fedka's promptings became more urgent. "It has become an occasion of sin. We must leave." With what seemed to Volkov great reluctance, the starets finally rose. He made his excuses to Koltso who only nodded, absorbed as he already was in pulling one of the women onto his lap. Volkov motioned Mitka to rise.

"It is best if we left now ourselves; we will escort Otyets Yakov to his lodging. It is late and I for one would rather spend the night in my own bed. You will be safer with us," he added, addressing the starets. For once Fedka nodded approval and even managed a crippled sort of smile.

"Yes, yes, it will be safer," he echoed. Absorbed in the women or close to drunken stupors, the Cossacks only made desultory gestures of farewell.

Outside the cold air stung Volkov's overheated cheeks but also came as something of a relief. He became more alert and saw gratefully that the snow had ceased. Mitka ordered their escort to leave the fire and the small troop was soon under way. The starets and his disciple were left at a nearby monastery where they had a night's lodging. Volkov and Mitka continued on to their own destination.

"We left the party too soon; it was just getting good," complained the bailiff.

"It's my duty to deliver you safely to your good wife," laughed Volkov. "And I, well, I didn't really didn't want to go to bed beside those fellows. Besides, leaving early gave us a chance to see the starets and his Fedka safely home."

"But, Gosudar, when drink goes in, sorrows go out."

"Of everything good, a little is better," countered Volkov.

Mitka thought the matter over, finally shrugging, "You are right, Gosudar, and it is after all one's own bed that warms best."

CHAPTER ELEVEN

Half obscured by shadow, long legs stretched out in front of him, Volkov sat staring seemingly at nothing. Disquieted by his silence which had gone on for most of the evening, Sofya attempted to stir his interest with tales of their children but even when he finally turned in her direction his thoughts still seemed centered elsewhere though he nodded dutifully now and then. She gave it up and concentrated instead on her needlework, laying it aside only when her eyes grew weary from working in the poor light cast by the flickering rushes.

"Serezhenka, I'm tired; it's time to go to bed."

"Yes," he replied, but made no move to rise.

"Of what can you be thinking? You have been far from this room all evening."

"Thinking? Oh, of any number of things."

"The murders perhaps?"

"Those among other matters." Since he was not

going to be more forthcoming, Sofya shrugged and left for bed herself.

Rivalries at court that could affect his position, small disturbances in the district, the latter the result of too much celebrating, and of course his unsolved murders had all gone through his head during the course of the evening. "Pugachev has hung his murderer. I have yet to find mine," he grumbled. "We shall have to begin questioning folk all over again." He determined to reinstitute just such an inquisition the following day.

"And you shall visit everyone in the neighborhood again," Volkov ordered his bailiff. "Take two men with you. I particularly want this man caught." He couldn't decide whether the urge for a solution was because he sought justice or because Pugachev's success where he'd failed, nettled him. "On your first inquiries, I presume, you not only asked if anyone unusual had been seen in the neighborhood but in fact obtained a list of anyone unusual that the residents of the area noticed on the day of the murder. And remember to ask about a possible sighting of the Cossacks as well." Volkov had originally contemplated a comparison of persons seen in the area of the murders and in both districts. That seemed ridiculous now that Pugachev had hung his culprit, yet---.

In any case, Volkov finally decided, the extra work wouldn't hurt his bailiff. Also knowing the comings and goings of certain citizens might prove useful at some time or other.

"Yes, Sudar. I asked, 'did you see a stranger in

the neighborhood who might have committed this crime'?"

"Phrase your question differently this time," ordered Volkov exasperated with Mitka, "or you'll have the citizens you interview imagining some fellow that looks like gallows bait and they'll shake their heads in denial. No one ever dreams of suspecting someone harmless in appearance, a priest say, or some substantial merchant. Just ask who they saw that day, known or unknown, ill-looking or even saintly for that matter. Store the list up there," said Volkov pointing to Mitka's head, "then bring it back to me. We'll sift through the information together." With a gesture the bailiff was dismissed and Volkov turned his attention to his other duties. "Fuck," he grumbled sifting through the petitions on the table in front of him, "these continuous accusations by one citizen of another for petty insults and breaches of the peace. We are assuredly a most litigious society. The palace has its hands full dealing with such disputes among the boyars and I have my hands full with everyone else." So with the exception of a brief visit to a kabak, Volkov spent the rest of the day on these matters until he left for home.

Early the next morning when he returned to his headquarters, Mitka was waiting, hat in hand, to report his findings. "Anything of significance?" asked Volkov.

"Perhaps."

"Sit down. Let's both be comfortable. Who has been named?"

Mitka mentioned the folk that had been seen in the neighborhood on the day of the murder. "Crown officials, Sudar. Not likely suspects, of course, and indeed, they were only coming and going. And someone saw the Shuisky entourage pass to and fro. Numerous merchants going about their business. Of some I have the names. Others were at least familiar to the locals. Shoppers of course. Workers going about their tasks. Priests. Streltsy as well." Then Mitka paused so long a moment that in exasperation Volkov bade him continue. Grinning, he added, "Our friends the Cossacks were there, sightseeing, the folk seemed to think." The bailiff leaned back against the wall the self-satisfied grin still on his face. "Now there's a possibility."

"I have to agree."

"Also the starets and his disciple," he continued more dismissively.

Volkov leaned forward. "What! Who saw them? When? Where exactly?"

"Why," replied Mitka, somewhat startled by Volkov's sudden eagerness to know, "any number of folk saw the two of them. Some even asked for a blessing." Volkov sat back brooding for some moments. "Shall I still find out about the Cossacks, Gosudar?"

"Yes, yes, that, as you've said, is at least a possibility. I'm sure they've all harassed women at one time or another. And as we've seen assault as well." They both recalled the kabak. "But murder here in Moscow? Since they're housed in the Kitaigorod, see if any of them could possibly have strayed into our district on the night in question. They weren't closely guarded until after my complaint and that was after the murders. Ask their keeper. See what he knows. But be subtle, remember they are the guests of the state. Say that this is on another matter entirely. Surely you can invent some excuse for your inquiry, eh?" Mitka nodded, saluted, and left. "Mitka's eager to catch the Cossacks but I'm actually more interested in the whereabouts of the starets that day." He rammed a fist against his forehead. "What is it between us, this man and me?"

His ruminations on the matter were cut short when Luka, excitement written all over his countenance, burst in on him without even asking leave. "My Lord, there's been still another murder of a young woman." Volkov rose at once.

"Where?"

"In our district," replied Luka, attempting at the same to dampen his excitement with an expression of sorrow for the deceased. Then he stood awestruck while his master let loose a string of vituperation that outclassed anything he'd ever heard before.

After he calmed down, Volkov asked, "Have you been to the site?"

"No, no, the matter was just reported," he said nodding towards the door. "A strelets was stopped in the street and came here as fast as his feet could carry him."

"Get our mounts and order out some of the men as well," growled Volkov. "And get a mount for our guide." Lest the Magistrate's obviously roused anger fall on him, Luka hastened to do his bidding. As their horses' hooves clattered down the planked streets, children were hurriedly whisked aside by fearful mothers, shoppers clung in terror to doorsills and gates, and wagon drivers did their best to maneuver aside. Continuing to use shouted threats and to flaunt their weapons as an incentive to get past the traffic in the streets, they made good time on their way to the neighborhood where the crime had been committed.

"Here, Sudar. This is the place," called out the accompanying strelets, reining in the mount that had been loaned to him. "Somewhere hereabouts citizens stopped me and sent me on to fetch you." As the troop came to a standstill, several men came out into the thoroughfare and pointed down a narrow lane.

"Gosudar, the murder, it was this way," one of the men, an older fellow, cried out.

Dismissing the strelets, Volkov and his men dismounted, leaving their horses in the care of several of the locals. Then the entire troop followed the beckoning elder. Except for the surroundings the scene is only too familiar, thought Volkov. A small white-washed church instead of a wayside shrine and lying on the ground next to it, a body. A young man knelt at the side of the victim, wailing. A priest, presumably the one who belonged to the church, was attempting to console him.

"Who is that?" asked Volkov.

"The husband," answered the most outspoken of their guides. Volkov looked more closely at the speaker. Noticing the glance, he introduced himself, "I am one of the elders hereabouts. When the body was discovered, I was summoned and it was I that immediately sent for the law."

"Then I shall need speak to you later, but first---," and Volkov gestured towards the dead woman. Luka following at his heels, he thrust his way through the inevitable crowd of curious onlookers and approached the body of the victim and her grieving husband. Except that this young woman was laid out neatly on the ground, it was like the scene a month ago.

"Strangled?" ventured Luka, and after a quick examination, Volkov nodded.

"Who found the body?" he called out. A short stumpy old man was pushed forward by the elder and Volkov took him aside so that the husband wouldn't overhear their remarks. "When did you find the body?"

"Early this morning, Gosudar. I was looking for my dear little dog. He seems to have disappeared and as we are old friends I was concerned for him. I still haven't found the poor fellow and there's no telling what could have happened to him."

"Yes, yes," interrupted Volkov, "but I have other concerns. Explain how you found the body."

"Well, Master, I am an old fellow as you can see and had to stop for a pee. I didn't want to take a leak right out in the lane where everyone could see so I went around to the side of the church. And there was the body. Out of the way it was and not easy to see. Besides my sight isn't what it used to be." To make his point, he squinted at Volkov, who impatiently gestured for him to continue. "As I got closer there she was, propped up against the church wall." The old man had kept his eyes averted from the body and he closed them completely at this point in his story. After adding a shudder, he leaned closer, dropping his voice to a whisper, "Her skirts were pulled up. I think, you know, that she'd been tampered with. That was too bad so I pulled down her skirts. She was a good lass too, always with a kind word for everyone and deserved a bit of dignity. I went to the elder at once to report the murder and he sent someone to tell her husband."

"Are any other of her family here?"

"Yes, Gosudar, both her in-laws and her family. The poor bereaved souls. I know them all. They are of this neighborhood."

"Point out the in-laws." The old man pointed to an older couple hovering over the lamenting husband. Substantial in appearance, the father was obviously shaken by the murder and his wife was in tears. Volkov motioned them forward. "Is this your daughter-in-law?" he asked.

"Yes, our sweet Varinka."

"When did she go missing?"

"Last night, my Lord," answered the man.

"And you didn't look for her?"

The man's face changed to one of indignation. "What do you take us for, my Lord, of course we looked. With lanterns we went back and forth and up and down all the lanes. My son was quite distraught. We couldn't imagine where she was."

"Why was she out so late?"

"It wasn't late. Only towards dusk. And she'd only gone to the home of her parents to borrow something for the kitchen. Something that you had to have, eh, woman," he complained, turning to his wife. "It couldn't wait until morning. And you had to send the girl." The woman's tears which had dried up in awe of the magistrate now flowed more abundantly than before and she began to pull at her clothes. "When it was dark, why we thought soon she'll come with her brother along for protection. When she still didn't return, my son went to retrieve her. Her people said she'd left some time before. Then we, all of us, searched the neighborhood from her old home to ours. But nothing of her did we see. None of us slept last night for the worry."

"Obviously you didn't search the side of the church."

"Why would we look there, Sudar?" he asked in surprise. "It is nowhere near the path she would have taken home. I cannot think how she got so far away. Who would do such a thing, Sudar? And her a young mother, too. What is my son to do now without a mother for his child? And without someone to warm his bed? "

"It must have been a demon," whispered his wife. The couple crossed themselves. "It was surely the evil one's work."

"Undoubtedly, but in the person of a man," said Volkov.

"Were there any strangers hereabouts yesterday or anytime recently?"

"Here? In our neighborhood? No, not that I can recall," answered the man.

"Have you any man here who has a reputation for bothering the women?"

The man appeared startled by the suggestion. "Here we live soul to soul, Sudar. We all know one another and get along pretty well. There is no one like that here. Why if there were, we'd take care of him fast enough." And the man waved a fist forcefully in the air.

"Then someone, perhaps just passing through of whom the women may have complained?" The man just shook his head. Volkov sighed. "Well, think about it. I shall question you again. You may as well take the body for burial." He bent towards the man. "Whoever sees to the body, must examine her for rape. And I shall need to speak to that person. I have to know these things you understand." He narrowed his eyes and snarled his last sentence to show he meant business.

"Yes, yes," the man agreed before Volkov strode away.

"Just like the other murder?" asked Luka.

"Yes, similar. And this business of putting the body near a church or a shrine has to mean something, though only God knows what. Did you find any footprints? I saw you looking while I was questioning the victim's in-laws."

Luka nodded over his shoulder towards the neighbors still gathered to commiserate with the bereaved and to gossip about the event. "I looked, we have dozens to choose from, all well-trodden ."

"Look some more. Go over the entire area with our men. See if the snow shows anything at all coming and going to the church." Volkov glanced at the sky. "At least it isn't snowing. I'm grateful it's cloudy and not so cold. Of course a biting wind might have kept this crowd from gathering and obliterating everything."

"Ah, Sudar, they would just have bundled up more warmly. You know how folk are; they don't want to miss anything. I think she wasn't dragged, you know. Her skirts are wet and in disarray but they are not particularly dirty. She was probably carried." Volkov waved him to continue with his search, detaching one man from the guard to question the onlookers and then to send them on their way. The girl's parents, he approached himself.

"I am sorry about your daughter."

"Sudar," pleaded the tearful father, "my wife is

near collapse. Please allow her to return to our home with my sons." Volkov agreed after stating that he would question them later and two young men and a young girl helped their mother home. Turning back to the magistrate, the man vowed to tell all he knew. "It isn't much. But I do want to find this fiend," he said, as he clenched and unclenched his fists. "She was a happy girl, our Varinka. A new mother too. And Yasha was a doting husband; you see how he weeps. One cannot fault him. His people are good folk too."

"You daughter came to your home on an errand yesterday?'

"Yes, and left with a basketful of dried mushrooms. But she didn't need a lantern. I thought, there's still plenty of light. Ah, I should have sent one of her brothers with her. But, you see, it's such a little way and we have no bad folk around here. We all know one another. Surely this is the work of some evil demon." The man's voice edged with fear, dropped to a whisper. "One hears of such things. Women stolen away by leshy."

"Uncle, you have no forest here. No place for a leshy to dwell. Understand, this crime was done by a man, not some forest spirit. Now, can you recall anyone new in the neighborhood?" The man shook his head. In exasperation Volkov turned to the priest he'd seen bending over the bereaved spouse. "Otyets, I must ask you some questions."

"Yes, Magistrate, please if I can help," he declared loudly, adding at once, "but I saw nothing and heard nothing." He pointed to his house some distance away on the opposite side of the church. "This is a terrible, terrible. What fiend would desecrate a church in this manner? And it was only yesterday honored by the presence of the starets, Otyets Yakov, lately come to our city. Surely you know of him, Sudar? I have a cousin who is an aide to the Metropolitan and he recommended me to that good man." The priest completely forgetting the murder, preened at the honor that had been bestowed upon him. "My wife made a feast, a real feast for our honored guest. Why, we had any number of dishes to serve, all of them prepared to perfection. The elders of the neighborhood came and the starets spoke to us all."

At the mention of the starets, Volkov's eyes had widened and the priest looking up at him appeared momentarily taken aback by their strange yellow glint. "How late did your honored guest stay? Perhaps he saw something?"

"It was just before dark. Of course he had a pass from the Metropolitan himself. And that man of his had a lantern. I offered to put him up in my own humble dwelling for the night but he said he had nothing to fear from anyone abroad at that hour. Surely he couldn't have seen anything, Gosudar. Why, he is such a man as would not leave someone in distress."

"Did you or your family see or hear any unusual in the night?"

No, we have discussed this among ourselves and we did not."

As Volkov dismissed the priest, all sorts of strange thoughts began tumbling through his head. Luka approached and he shook off the lunatic notions he'd been entertaining, and asked, "Have you found anything?"

"Footprints that sank deeply into the snow as if under a great weight."

"Going from where to where?"

"To the church from a stall holding a single horse not too far away."

"Show me this stall. Let's see if it was the scene of the crime. Did you find a basket of mushrooms?"

"No, I came back to find you. Some fellow, the owner of the horse, I think, confronted me with an axe and I decided to get assistance."

"Get the rest of the men then and we shall confront him."

The footprints that were exceptional in how deeply they sank into the crusted snow without however defining what size of foot made them, went on some distance. The prints were made by boots though, I think, not bast shoes," commented Luka.

"Is this the route the girl had to follow to get from her parents' home to the home of her in-laws?"

Luka shook his head. "Rather out of the way, Sudar. But here is the stall."

The entire troop massed in the man's minuscule yard churning up the snow, quickly leaving the premises dismal and dirty. Standing in the doorway of the small stall, the proprietor was still defiantly waving his axe. "My men could take you down in a minute so drop your weapon, you foolish fellow," Volkov called out to him. Before he could say anything further, a disheveled woman ran in front of him, waving her arms frantically and shouting.

"My man did nothing. He is innocent."

"I am not accusing him, auntie. Tell him to lay

down his weapon. We only want to see the inside of the stall. But if we cannot do this, then it shall become the worse for him."

"Ah, Borya, do as the Magistrate says. What can you do against so many?" The man appeared obstinate for a few moments more then put down the axe.

He punched himself in the chest. "I may look like a sheep's coat to you but I am a human like yourself. And I defend what's mine." Volkov brushed by the man, eager to see inside the stall while Luka continued to remonstrate with the owner of what proved to an aged broken down nag. In a corner Volkov noted a broken basket its contents of dried mushrooms spread pitifully among the disturbed pile of straw.

"The girl's," he said to Luka, pointing.

"Hey you, what do you know about the young mother that was murdered near the church?" shouted Luka. "Yes, what do you know," he repeated, jabbing the man's chest with this finger. The man looked around in confusion, sputtering denials against the accusation. It was obvious he was shaken. His wife came to the door of the stall and when she heard of what he was accused she grew hysterical.

"My man did nothing," she cried over and over again as she kept wringing her hands.

"I should be the one to complain here," said the householder who while he continued to protest his innocence also began whining about the disturbance to his property. "The straw has been scattered all over the stall. The horse blanket I found outside. My horse, Gosudar, see he's been upset; my old darling may never be good for anything again." Volkov looked at the sorry old beast who oblivious to the stir was calmly chewing at the grain in his bin.

"He seems to be taking the excitement in his stride," commented Volkov in a voice tinged with sarcasm. "Where were you last night?"

"Asleep in my bed, as any good Christian ought to be," firmly declared the man.

"How many in your household?"

"My wife," he replied, pointing to the sobbing woman standing in the yard. "Two sons, a daughter, a daughter-in-law, and my aged mother."

"Where are they?"

"Still in the house, afraid to venture out," he answered, pointing to the door where the others were hovering, the aged parent in the front. "Yes, they can all vouch for me. We all sleep in the same room. I will swear it on the cross for you. I will swear it twenty times."

"And this?" Volkov nudged the broken basket with the toe of his boot.

The man shook his head violently. "It's not mine. I know nothing about it."

"You two stay out here," Volkov ordered the couple. To Luka he said, "Question the others in the household," adding sarcastically, "and see if what he's willing to swear to so many times is verified by them. I shall go back to the murder site and investigate further there. Come and report to me when you're done here." Another man he delegated to look for further footprints.

Sometime later Luka reported back to the church where he found the magistrate conferring with an elder. Volkov gestured for Luka to wait. From the expression on his face he seemed to be hearing something of interest. The two men were not attempting to lower their voices so Luka leaned forward to catch the information that was being exchanged.

"So you say that this fellow was a stranger to the district?"

"Yes, one such as I have never seen before. What could his sort be doing in our neighborhood, I asked myself. We are small traders and craftsmen here. We sell in the markets. This fellow looked like a brigand." He shrugged. "Though to be sure he may have been a peaceable enough fellow. But, Sudar, the way he held himself, his scowl, why, they indicated something else entirely. And he saw me but made no inquiries." The elder paused to give the matter more thought. "I think the fellow knew his destination." He shook his head in puzzlement. He was most definitely out of place. After he disappeared from sight, I put him out of my mind until now."

"Tell me more about his appearance. Was he a Tatar? A Circassian? Perhaps a Pole?"

"No, Sudar, by his clothes, he was Rus but a rough looking fellow for sure."

"And this was the only stranger you saw hereabouts?"

"Yes." The elder stroked his beard thoughtfully. Volkov noted that something else seemed to be troubling him but over this he hesitated to speak. "There's another matter troubling you, isn't there?"

The man nodded. "Sudar, I overheard you question old Guryev, the victim's father-in-law. He told you that we had no one hereabouts who bothered the womenfolk. That is true, Yet---" He stopped.

"Go on, go on. Don't be hesitant. I need to know anything that can help me find this fiend."

"I don't wish to make trouble for Foma or his mother." Volkov frowned sternly at the man and he continued. "We have a young man living here, Sudar. A simple fellow. One that can do only very simple tasks. A heavy burden really to his poor mother for she must see to him constantly as he is forever straying off. Oh, he is a big strong fellow but in his mind, he is like a child. And---"

"And?"

"He follows the young women. A few have complained to their menfolk and they have come to me. They know he is simple. But he is so big and strong and for that reason he frightens the more timid. But, Sudar, he has never assaulted anyone. Still, in the light of what has happened," and he nodded back towards the church, "I felt I had to tell you."

"It was your duty to do so. I shall question him."

The elder shrugged. "He won't be much help."

"Then I shall interrogate his family and his neighbors. Give my man here directions to his dwelling. Luka, you've been listening. Here is someone for us to question." Turning back to the elder he thanked him then waited while, with much finger pointing and gesturing, directions were given in the one case and absorbed in the other. Afterwards the elder retreated to his own home. Motioning Luka closer he asked, "What of that belligerent fellow and his family? Did he speak the truth?"

"Afraid they were when I questioned them,

Sudar. They shook in every limb. But the whole family stoutly insists that the father was safely asleep in his bed and stayed there. It seems the householder, the wife, and the old woman have the best places near to and on the stove and would have had difficulty leaving as the rest of the family sleep between the stove and the door. One of the sons says his father grunts like a pig in his sleep and that as usual he was grunting last night. Sudar, they're probably speaking the truth. It's pretty frightened they were. Timid souls in contrast to the old father."

"So all we know this time is where the girl was murdered but who—? And the church is not convenient to the stable yet the murderer took the trouble to carry the victim there. As I said before, this has to have some significance." His voice dropped. "Or at least so I believe." He stood in silence for what to Luka seemed a long while. Then he shook off whatever was bothering him and announced, "Let us go and question this simple fellow and his mother."

Someone must have warned the old mother for she was already standing in the doorway of her home, arms crossed, a heavy frown on her face when Volkov and his men arrived. "My son is one of God's innocents. He has done nothing," she growled.

"Nonetheless we will question him. Let us in, I do not want to shout my questions out here in the cold." He motioned to his men and they all moved closer in a most intimidating manner. Her face crumpled. She dropped her hands and after a long pause finally stepped back into the room. Volkov ordered his men to stay in the yard; he and Luka entered the small house. The woman began to shake and Volkov put a hand on her shoulder willing her to be calm.

"Foma was with me all night. He did no one any harm," she protested. Volkov looked around at the meagerly furnished room. A great lout of a fellow was sitting peaceably enough at the table. His mother went to him and lay her hands protectively on his shoulders.

"Stand up," ordered Volkov. The young man merely gaped back at the magistrate. Volkov repeated his request.

"Get up for the lord, Foma." The fellow rose. "See how he behaves, Gosudar. He is a good boy." Volkov noted his size.

"A big fellow," whispered Luka, "he could easily have lifted the woman and carried her to the church. And his hands, look at them, Sudar, like great haunches of meat."

"Ah, Sudar," wailed the mother, "he was here all night, all evening."

"Are you two the only ones who live here?"

"Yes, Lord."

"Then we have only your word."

"But I know he has done nothing. He is harmless. My neighbors will tell you the same."

"We shall ask them. I've already been told that he follows women and frightens them."

"Ah, if he followed them, it is because he likes to be with people. The lads they tease him but the women they are more kind. Go and ask, he has never laid hands on anyone."

Volkov looked at the young man. "Foma, tell me. Do you know Varvara Guryeva?" He received an answering grin, a rather foolish one. Finally after looking to his mother and seeming to get her approval, he nodded. "Did you see her last night?" Now the simpleton's expression seemed to be straining at something. Finally he shook his head. Volkov decided to give it up. He motioned for Luka to withdraw. Outside he told him, "Stay and question the neighbors. The mother's testimony is naturally biased and can be discounted. Her neighbors will be more disinterested. See what they have to say. I'm inclined to believe her. Placing the body near the church took some thought and seems beyond what Foma can do. Yet---? And as for the rest of the men. Ask about the rough-looking fellow as well. A Cossack, perhaps? In any case, I shall return to headquarters. Report to me there."

When Volkov returned he found Mitka waiting for him and informed him of the latest murder. The bailiff shook his head at the enormity of it all. "What of the Cossacks?" Volkov asked as he removed his heavy coat and handed it to a clerk. "Out," he growled and shut the door which usually remained open in the clerk's face.

"Home dead drunk on the nights in question, says their keeper. He says they suck in enough each evening to fill a small pond and then sleep like the dead."

Mention of drinking reminded Volkov of his own thirst and he opened the door to demand some mead. Afterwards he turned back to his bailiff. "Can we be sure their warder wasn't in the same state? Can he account for everyone each of the evenings in question?"

"Sudar, this is one great worrier. He feels if he doesn't account for them every moment, he will be held personally responsible by the tsar himself. But until you complained after the damage to the kabak, why I think, he may well have taken his duty more lightly. So it's possible for one or more of them to have slipped away as there were no guards."

"A fellow that looked like some frontier brigand was seen in the vicinity of last night's murder. But was it one of our Cossacks? After all the city is filled with the Tsar's mercenaries. An elder, though, swears that the clothing was nothing exotic and this stranger was one of us." Volkov looked disgruntled. "This time we have a surfeit of suspects." And for Mitka's benefit, he described the local simpleton who had the habit of following girls.

"Did you learn about anyone else suspicious besides the Cossacks? Surely you have something else to report?" Mitka opened his mouth to speak when a knock sounded at the door.

"Come in," called Volkov. The returning clerk, pale and frightened, held out a tray with a pitcher and two mugs. Mitka took it and kicked the door shut. He poured for both of them, smiling as he did. He'd sensed the ambivalent feelings his master held about the starets. Putting a finger to the side of his nose and closing one eye, he tried to look shrewd.

"I asked considerably more about the starets. Yes, I tracked the fellow to where he'd resided that evening. It was at one of the monasteries close by. I questioned the gate-keeper, a querulous fellow, thank the Lord. He made it easy for me to learn things. I said I greatly admired the starets. They have an especially fine healer at that particular monastery, one well-versed in all manner of herbal remedies. It was him the starets was visiting. Yes, Otyets Yakov comes and goes in the

evening with no problem, he and that Fedka." Volkov's
eyes had narrowed during Mitka's tale. "You're on the
scent of something, eh, Sudar?"

"Perhaps." He said nothing further for some time.
Mitka forced to wait patiently, heaved great sighs every
few moments of which his master took no notice. Finally
Volkov broke the silence.

"I want you to make certain discreet inquiries.
Very discreet inquiries. We could get into difficulties if
you are not careful, more than if we seek information
about the Cossacks, about whom in any case officials
might readily believe the worst. And if through
carelessness I find myself in difficulty, let me tell you
right now, I shall make problems for you. Do you
understand?" Mitka nodded, his eyes wide open. He
leaned forward to catch every word. "You are to find out
not just where the starets spent the evening of the first
murder but when he left his hostel and when he returned
and if possible in what condition. And you are to do the
same for the murder in the Skorodom." Mitka's mouth,
what could be seen of it between the forest of his beard
and mustache, gaped in surprise. In spite of trying to
please Volkov by inquiring about the starets'
whereabouts, this went further than he'd imagined. "Yes,
I want to know where the starets was then as well. And
add last night's whereabouts as well. Indeed, begin with
last night. Ask the priest there; since he was close by last
evening we have the excuse that the starets might be able
to help us in our inquiries. I don't want to do it myself. It
might make his various hosts attach too much
significance to the questions. I want it to seem as routine
and ordinary an inquiry as possible.

"And your lies had better be plausible.
Remember this man is sanctioned by the Metropolitan
himself. And the church is very sensitive as to its
reputation and its rights and privileges. So be subtle, lie,
of course, but don't overdo it."

"And the Cossacks?"

"Ah, yes, our friends, the reformed brigands.
When Luka returns from his hunt he can investigate their
whereabouts more closely. Yet, I do not see a Cossack
laying out his victims and leaving them at a church or
shrine." He laughed. But it was a nasty laugh that boded
ill for someone thought Mitka, hopefully he prayed, not
himself. "Meanwhile find out what you can and we'll see
if a certain someone can come out of the water dry."

CHAPTER TWELVE

Frustrated by waiting in the outer reception chamber of the Metropolitan's palace, Volkov tried to ease his restlessness by returning measure for measure the suspicious gazes of the various clerics passing to and fro as they went about their tasks. Since being summoned for an interview with Metropolitan Antoniye, he'd braced himself against the worst. "Mitka did not tread carefully enough," he sighed, wishing himself elsewhere. As a last resort he sought distraction in the faces of the holy saints covering the frescoed walls but the haughty expressions of resident clerics prevented his finding any solace in dead apostles and martyrs. For that matter there was little or no solace to be found in the stern painted faces. Gradually as his unease turned to anger at the deliberate delay, the clergy in their long black cassocks became the object of his scorn.
"Carrion crows," he sneered, "waiting to pick over still

another carcass."

After the long and dreary wait, the door to the inner chamber finally opened and still another cleric emerged. "The Metropolitan will see you now," he announced grandly, and with a gesture insulting in its brevity, motioned Volkov forward. The magistrate entered a sumptuous chamber filled with icons, jeweled crosses, and precious reliquaries. Metropolitan Antoniye was seated in a raised chair at the end of the room nearest the stove. In an illusion of splendor created by his costly regalia, a high-crowned hat adding necessary stature, the otherwise squat and unprepossessing figure beckoned Volkov forward. The magistrate, hat in hand, bowed so low, his forehead touched the floor. Antoniye deliberately kept him in this pose for some moments. When he finally bade him rise, he indicated a bench with his staff and Volkov seated himself. He kept his face expressionless while the Metropolitan examined him but inwardly he seethed.

"I have to sweep the floor for this toady, this pithless creature of the tsar's." He felt some satisfaction in the fact the Antoniye had to humble himself in just such a way to Ivan. "Everyone knows that he doesn't have the balls to naysay the tsar even on matters of theology. Indeed, the fellow was selected for just that reason. No, our Prince doesn't like opposition even from the chief prelate in all of Rus." With disdain he surveyed the man's soft hands and weak features.

"Do you know why we have called you here, Magistrate?" the man asked, breaking into Volkov's uncomplimentary thoughts.

"I have no suspicion, Holiness."

"You should, for you have gone beyond your jurisdiction. News has reached us that you are investigating our honored guest, the starets, Yakov. And, though we find this almost impossible to believe, in connection with the murders of some young women. How dare you? How presumptuous of you! How could you possibly have connected this worthy man to such heinous crimes?" Volkov opened his mouth to reply but Antoniye held up his hand. "Not yet, Magistrate, we are not finished. The starets is as I said a good man. We have declared it to be so. Why, he comes to us from Nizhni Novgorod with an excellent report from the bishop of that town. He has prostrated himself before us. We were impressed with the humility displayed by this worthy man. Abbots and bishops in distant parts speak well of his works in healing and preaching. In this wicked world such a man is needed. No, Magistrate, he is a fine representative of Holy Rus."

"Yes," thought Volkov, as the Metropolitan continued to heap praise on the starets, "but the devil always comes dressed in the latest fashion."

"A humble son of the soil," Antoniye went on, "yet he has impressed us with his powers."

Volkov sighed. He had to admit that the starets puzzled him as well. There were contradictions in the man. Yet he continued to feel that there was a dark side to the starets and after all it was his duty to investigate the murders. Murders that were beginning to disrupt his district. He was abruptly recalled to what the Metropolitan was saying for the man's voice had risen still higher, becoming shrill and decidedly unpleasant.

"We order you to cease your investigation of the

starets at once. Do you hear Magistrate?"

Volkov tried to explain himself but the Metropolitan raised a hand to silence him. "So I'm to get no hearing at all," he fumed silently. "The man won't hear a word against the starets. He's become inviolate."

"If this persecution of the starets continues, we shall have to inform the palace." A few questions are hardly a persecution, thought Volkov. Narrowing his eyes and tightening his lips, he couldn't help looking at the prelate with scorn. Correctly interpreting his expression, the Metropolitan appeared taken aback and his voice fell away.

"What a timid creature this is. Yes," thought Volkov, "perhaps he's suddenly remembered Metropolitan Filip who was dragged from his church, exiled to a remote monastery, then smothered in his cell, all on the orders of the tsar. Does this fellow really want to call attention to himself by whining into Ivan's ear? I rather doubt it. Still, if I push him, he may get up sufficient courage to defend church privileges and do I want to risk that? I think not." He sighed again and that gave Antoniye enough resolution to end the interview on a high note for himself.

"The starets does not know of your investigation. It came to our attention through other sources. Do not trouble that good man any further in this." He cleared his throat and raised his voice, "You are dismissed, Magistrate." Volkov rose, bowed low, and left the room. Striding through the outer chamber, he gazed neither to the right nor to the left. He was not about to give the curious clerics any satisfaction and be further humiliated.

His ride back to his headquarters was accelerated

by a mounting fury. He strode past instantly cautious clerks with an expression they knew boded ill for someone. "Mitka! Where is Mitka?" he shouted, revealing the source of his anger. Various looks passed among the clerks, relief that it wasn't one of them that was the object of Volkov's fury, a modicum of sympathy for the culprit, and continued caution least they divert attention to themselves instead. They immediately withdrew into a close and politic scrutiny of the papers lying in front of them.

"Here I am," cried the bailiff, coming on the run.

"Inside," ordered Volkov. Mitka rushed ahead in order to open the door of the inner office. When they were inside, Volkov kicked it shut and launched into a tirade. "I warned you, did I not, to be discreet, to exercise caution. Well, the Metropolitan himself has just ordered me, and in no uncertain terms, to keep my hands off of Father Yakov." Volkov gave Mitka a clout on the ear that set his head to ringing. "It seems Antoniye approves of him. The starets is now as sacred as any reliquary. How could you allow this to happen?" He gave Mitka a clout on the other ear. "How did our foremost prelate learn of the investigation? Should I have sent Luka instead?" Mitka was affronted by this reference to his rival. A look of consternation came over his face and momentarily he forgot about his ears. "Should I perhaps have undertaken this investigation myself and interviewed monastic gatekeepers, domestics, and the like? Well, I'm waiting to hear what you have to say?"

"Ah, Gosudar, I thought everything was going well," pleaded Mitka. Tentatively feeling first one ear then the other, he made an effort to stand at attention. "Why, I tracked that fellow and his flunky from here to the Skorodom and back again. Hours and hours it took me. And in the biting cold," he concluded with a deep sigh. Volkov dismissed his suffering with a glare and waved him to go on. "I know where he took shelter and when. I can't imagine how the Metropolitan came to hear of the investigation. No one, I assure you, gave me the least indication that my lies weren't plausible. Why, on one occasion, I was even wined and dined."

"Hah, that is undoubtedly when you gave yourself away," retorted Volkov. "Everyone knows that what's on a sober man's mind is on a drunken man's tongue."

"No, no, Gosudar," wailed Mitka, holding out his hands in supplication. "Have you ever seen me fail in this regard? I can hold my drink. I know my limit." His look changed as if he'd had a sudden inspiration. "Why, perhaps, it is the starets himself." His voice fell to a whisper. "Yes, that is it." Mitka shrugged and threw up his hands. "What can I do against such powers."

"You dolt. That is nonsense. Such powers are given to saints and the starets is no saint."

"Ah, but Gosudar, the devil, he has powers too." Mitka crossed himself and murmured a brief prayer.

"Otyets Yakov is neither saint nor devil. But he is a man and therefore fallible. Besides the Metropolitan informed me that the complaint did not come from the starets, that indeed he knows nothing of our investigation." Volkov sat down, adding, "No, he had no vision of you tracking him. Somehow you failed. And as a result our search into his doings has to cease." His voice softened and Mitka thought the worst was over so he give the magistrate a weak grin. "Now, tell me what you did discover."

Relieved to be getting off lightly, since the tone of Volkov's voice now implied resignation rather than anger, Mitka rushed to tell all that he had learned. "As to our two murders, the starets was housed in our district on both occasions. As you know he was even in the vicinity on the night of the last strangulation. As to our poor snowmaiden---." Mitka's look grew more cunning. "Why, he was staying at a monastery near her neighborhood that night and the porter says he came in late. But the fellow couldn't remember more than that. And after all, Sudar, it was so long ago. But on the night of the little mother's murder, the gatekeeper says Otyets Yakov looked as if he were a thousand, thousand versts distant in some remote place only a raven could find. He didn't reply at all to the gatekeeper's good wishes which annoyed the old fellow no end and made him remember. He seemed distracted is what the fellow said. And that man of his, well, he was the same as always, surly and curt. Of course, I said, I'd come to speak to the starets in order to see if he could help me with the latest investigation since he'd been at a priest's residence nearby. Then what did that fool of a gatekeeper do but promptly dash off to get the starets for me. I didn't get a chance to say it could be put off until another day. So, Sudar, hat in hand, I had to go in and see the starets and his Fedka. I used the excuse of wanting to know if he'd seen anything. 'No,' he said, 'I saw nothing. I cannot help you for I heard no cries and saw no struggle.' And indeed, he seemed very sorry that he couldn't assist me.

That sword and shield of his, that Fedka, though looked as fierce as ever. I swear I felt the fellow might annihilate me on the spot. It was just as he looked that day in the square when the holy fool said those strange things to Otyets Yakov. Anyway, I thanked them both, bowed myself out, and went on to the Skorodom."

"And in the Skorodom?" Mitka reddened and Volkov narrowed his eyes in suspicion.

"Can you guess, Gosudar, where the starets was housed?"

"We are not playing at riddles here, you fool."

Mitka hurried to reply, "Once he was a guest of Magistrate Pugachev himself. Though he was invited elsewhere in the district as well. A commander of streltsy treated him to Advent fare as did the monks at one of the monasteries. Elders in the area bid for his presence too. He came and went freely is what I heard. On the night of Sveta's murder, I couldn't find out where he was but he was definitely in the same district. Discretion kept me from probing further," he concluded piously.

"I wonder if Pugachev found out what we were doing due to your bumbling. And if he did, would he betray me to the Metropolitan? Yes, he might, especially if he thought I was questioning his own findings in regard to Sveta's murder and its result. Ah, it's probably pointless now worrying about how it happened. Still, the next time I see Pugachev I will examine his countenance closely. Perhaps I'll owe him something in return."

"What's to do now?"

Volkov glared at him and Mitka stepped back a pace. "Do now? There's nothing we can do now." He waved Mitka away and the bailiff very quietly eased himself from the room leaving the magistrate to his own thoughts. Volkov sat down finally after pouring himself more mead. Musing over his relationship with the starets, he declared to the empty room, "I'm mad to pursue this man. Surely there are others as yet undiscovered who could have been in both districts on the relevant evenings. The uncouth fellow that the elder described is a possibility. Have I allowed my prejudice against Father Yakov to overcome my common sense?" He thought back to the hated starets of his youth. "Now he was a charlatan, of that I have no doubt." He remembered in particular one time when he'd been upbraided for his sins by the 'holy man' who then advised his father to take sterner measures in disciplining him. God, how he'd loathed that fellow. And truly this Yakov seems different. At times I find he's quite companionable. So many vouch for the fellow as well. Ah, Volkov give it up, look elsewhere. Don't be like the falcon who won't let go what it grabs in its claws." With that last comment to himself, Vokov pulled forward the papers the clerks had placed on the table for his perusal and began to study them.

CHAPTER THIRTEEN

After the meeting with the Metropolitan, Volkov concentrated on other affairs in his district though the murders continued to prey on his mind. People were demanding to see him eager to report suspicious strangers; still others came with tales of neighbors against whom they bore a grudge. Volkov was forced to spend considerable time sifting through the accusations and the sightings. As to the simpleton, his neighbors defended him though they admitted readily enough that his presence gave some of the more timorous women a bit of a fright. As for the Cossacks, they couldn't be placed at their residence with absolute certainty. Hauling them to headquarters when they were out of his jurisdiction however would have called the attention of the palace to himself. So Volkov, still smarting from the Metropolitan's reprimand, had Luka investigate them as discreetly as possible.

As to the starets, one day Volkov encountered the

man in the streets. It was as if nothing had happened to mar their acquaintance for Father Yakov greeted him with the utmost friendliness and it was almost more than the magistrate could bear. He mumbled to himself after the chance meeting, "Surely the devil is more dangerous when he comes as a dog wagging his tail then when he comes as a rushing bear." Then remembering how helpful the man had been and also his evident piety on occasion, Volkov again berated himself for being an obstinate fool.

Returning from that encounter to his office, Volkov came across a crowd milling about in the street and saw several of his own men involved in separating the chief combatants and their adherents. They, along with the eager onlookers were effectively blocking traffic, and carts were beginning to congregate because of the impasse. As he thrust back the avid onlookers, Volkov was seen by Luka who rushed over, crying out, "See, Sudar, these merchants are about to come to blows. One of them is accusing the other of theft and the accused says it is all a pack of lies. We were summoned and arrived not five minutes ago."

"Bring everyone concerned to headquarters. Leave a few of your men to clear the streets of this crowd; this sort of turmoil can't be allowed. Folk will surely disperse easily enough once the players in this drama have been taken away." Satisfied that his orders were being carried out, Volkov preceded all those involved back to his headquarters. Ordering refreshments and making himself comfortable, he waited for the combatants to arrive. Soon a large noisy party, jostling one another in their eagerness to have a say, made its way into his office. Well wrapped as they were against the cold outside in fur coats, hats, and mittens, the phalanx the antagonists presented took up considerable space. To bring order out of the continuing chaos, Volkov asked Luka if he knew what the conflict entailed. "The rest of you hold your tongues," he shouted, seeking to cow the small array of tradesmen into submission.

"I have some facts, Sudar. These tradesmen---".

"I am a merchant, Gosudar," interrupted a short, stout man, his raised beard quivering in indignation, "Matvey Lobachev, lately arrived in your city. And this knave," he sputtered, pointing to yet another solidly built specimen of the same class, "accuses me of theft. Me, that's known throughout the upper Volga for my honesty, the value of my goods, and for my---."

"Were you given leave to speak?" interrupted Volkov in a voice so cold that the merchant immediately sank into frustrated silence. "As you were about to say, Luka," he added, waving his subordinate into continuing.

"Yes, Sudar, this Matvey Lobachev," and Luka pointed to the indignant merchant who'd spoken up in his own defense, "has to been accused by Ziven Slepuchin of our own city of attempting to sell him stolen merchandise" Lobachev began to sputter again and Volkov had to quell him with still another cold look. "Lobachev denies this accusation as you can see."

"Slepuchin, on what basis do you accuse this man of theft?" demanded Volkov.

"Ah, Gosudar, I heard from a close colleague only this morning that he'd lost these same wares in the night and now see, this thief is trying to pass them off as his own. But, me, Slepuchin, I am not so easily taken in as that."

"What are the goods in question?"

"Imported leather goods," announced both merchants simultaneously. "The finest Moroccan leather," added Lobachev.

"Has this theft mentioned by Slepuchin been reported to us?" Volkov asked Luka.

"No, it has not, Sudar."

"Ah, my Lord, my poor friend probably never had the chance. But see, I myself have discovered the culprit. Me, Slepuchin," and he beat his chest in self-approbation.

"Lobachev, you may speak. What can you say in your defense?"

"I have witnesses who saw me unload my goods from sledges just yesterday and convey them to a warehouse where they were inventoried. This fool," said the accused merchant, nodding towards Slepuchin, "buys such goods for the local market and I conveyed a few of the items to him for sale. And see his response. It is all a pack of lies." He looked angry enough to pull out the beard of his opponent and leaning closer caused Slepuchin to withdraw a few paces. But a glance from Volkov made him ease off.

"Luka, have you sent for anyone else connected with this case?"

"I had no chance, Sudar," said Luka, spreading his hands in a plea for understanding.

"Well, do so now. Send for Slepuchin's friend, this fellow who's supposed to have lost some goods. And for Lobachev's witnesses as well. You know," he said turning to Lobachev, "you will need two or three good men to testify in your defense." The merchant nodded. "Give their names to my man here. Luka, is the merchandise in question here as well?" Luka said it was. "All of you will for the time being adjourn into the other room to wait." Nodding towards two other men who'd come in with the merchants, he asked, "Who are these other fellows?"

"That is my man, Volodika," replied Lobachev, pointing to a thin, hard-faced fellow, "come with me all the way from Nizhni Novgorod, where I chiefly reside."

"And this fellow?" Volkov indicated an obese youth, the image of Slepuchin.

"Pyotr, my son," answered the merchant in a tone of pride. Volkov acknowledged the answers with a nod at the same time waving them all into the next room to sit among his clerks. The effort the clerks put into their work came to a halt while they examined each of the opponents in turn and cocked their ears in order to hear as much of their murmurs and grumbles as they possibly could. Luka shut the door so Volkov could have privacy. He sat down and drank some of his mead.

"Hmm, Nizhni Novgorod," he mused aloud. "Where according to the Metropolitan the starets won acclaim. Let's hope this case of theft resolves itself easily, then I shall perhaps interview this Lobachev privately. He may have heard of Otyets Yakov." He shook his head bemused at his persistence in believing the worst of the starets. "So much for my resolution to leave the man in peace." Trying to put the annoying matter aside, he rose and called in a clerk to begin recording the facts of the case known thus far. After about two hours, Luka returned and announced the presence of all the witnesses.

"Herd them all in here then," ordered Volkov. Luka pushed back the benches and stools, then placed the antagonists against the wall at opposite ends of the room from one another. The two groups eyed one another suspiciously and mumbled softly among themselves. "Lobachev, introduce your witnesses." The merchant indicated three fellow traders, residents of Moscow.

"These are the men, my Lord. They saw me unload my goods and warehouse them. Since they expressed interest in purchasing some of the items, we unwrapped them in the warehouse so they could see the fine quality of all my leatherware."

Looking at the three men, Volkov nodded for them to give one of his clerks their names. One of them spoke up, "With your permission, Gosudar, I am sure that you recognize our names as we are prominent in business affairs hereabouts."

"Yes, indeed I do. Slepuchin, you'll agree that these are prominent tax-payers, good Christians, and therefore worthy witnesses?" Slepuchin nodded agreement but reluctantly, his expression showing that he thought his accusation was beginning to fray at the seams.

"Do you three gentlemen agree that these leather goods," and Volkov pointed to the items mentioned now reposing on the floor in front of the table he used as a desk, "belong to Lobachev and are not stolen items?"

The three witnesses carefully examined the goods, consulted with one another, and finally the one appointed as spokesman stated, "We would be willing to swear on the cross that these items belong to Lobachev and that he unloaded them from the sledges in our presence and later unwrapped these same goods in the warehouse also in our presence. And that further they are marked with his special mark." Lobachev seemed to grow in stature with each remark and he looked in triumph at his crestfallen opponent.

"What do you have to say?" Volkov asked Slepuchin.

"My friend reported goods just such as these stolen from the warehouse. What was I to think, my Lord?"

"Is your friend present?" Slepuchin nodded and pointed to still another merchant.

Indicating the goods, Volkov asked, "Are these or are they not your goods?"

The little man, the antithesis of a robust Moscow tradesman, looked closely at the goods in question, then in a voice like a cannon shot, cried out, "Ah, Ziv, what were you thinking of? These are not my things. You have made trouble for me unnecessarily."

"And didn't you lose just such items from your premises last evening?" Volkov demanded to know.

"It's true that I lost similar items to theft. But I was undertaking a search before reporting the loss. Not wishing to disturb you, my Lord," he added ingratiatingly, "without all the facts in hand."

"And has your search been completed?"

"No, Gosudar, we are still ascertaining the amount of loss."

Slepuchin turned beet red and began shouting at

his friend, "But you wrung your hands and then cried and cried over your losses to me this very morning. See the difficulties your whining has cost me."

"Ah, Ziv, it was the shock. Besides, how was I to know you would immediately accuse this worthy visitor of the theft." He turned and bowed to Lobachev.

"Lobachev, I most humbly apologize," said Slepuchin, turning with a simpering smile in the direction of his former antagonist.

Lobachev looked at him in disdain. "My good name has had a slur cast upon it. I should take you to court. I deserve compensation."

Volkov intervened. "Our courts are already overburdened with cases of besmirched honor. Settle this among yourselves now. The state has more important concerns." All the merchants in the room looked at Volkov as if he'd proposed something totally alien and he supposed he had. "I suggest a fine. Let Slepuchin compensate Lobachev." Slepuchin blanched. "And you," Volkov told his merchant friend, "shall bear a portion of the costs as well. You should have reported your losses to us instead of enlisting the assistance of your colleague. Lobachev would a reasonable fine satisfy you?"

"Yes, my Lord, after all I really have no time to waste here. After my goods are disposed of, I wish to go back to my own town. I am due to join a trading flotilla to Astrakhan to procure further merchandise in a few months and must prepare well in advance for that journey."

Volkov then proposed a figure that seemed so reasonable that some of the color returned to Slepuchin's countenance. Lobachev was not so pleased but his three Moscow colleagues urged him to accept and he finally nodded agreement. Volkov then dismissed everyone but Lobachev who appeared faintly puzzled by the delay.

"I have a few things to say to you and some questions to ask as well. I propose first that you join me in something to eat and drink. You man may join us as well. Please sit." Obviously curious about what was to happen, the merchant settled himself on a bench in front of Volkov's table while the magistrate ordered a repast to be brought in from a local kabak.

"First, Matvey Lobachev, I know that you were not completely satisfied with the monetary compensation but after all this is not your city and your reputation has not been seriously besmirched. In the end the whole affair was really only a minor inconvenience for you. It would have been a major inconvenience for all concerned including yourself had it gone on into the courts. Your friends here in Moscow, I believe, correctly urged you to accede to the fine. They have to live here; a heavier fine would have made for disharmony among these men, something I couldn't allow."

"Yes, Gosudar, I can understand that. Yes, that is reasonable. And I may wish to do business here on other occasions so it is well that I make no enemies." He laughed. "I'm a practical fellow and to indulge in these lawsuits over honor, well, I say, let the boyars do that if they have the time and the inclination."

"Would there were more people who thought as you do." Then Volkov asked Lobachev questions about his trading expeditions and the merchant answered readily. He had a good many adventures to relate from his journeys up and down the Volga and even to foreign lands such as Georgia and Persia, so that Volkov found him both knowledgeable and amusing.

"Yes, Sudar, I sell abroad our furs, our beeswax, as well as dry salted fish. And I return with the finest carpets and leatherwares. Sometimes with silks and incense too. Ah, it's great risks we take in our travels to bring these fine things to Rus. Why, there are floods in the spring, rains in the fall, and mud in both seasons. And brigands on the Volga. Add to this then, Magistrate, the necessity of dealing cleverly with foreign traders who naturally want to buy low and sell high. Yes, one needs courage and acumen to be in foreign trade." Volkov praised his efforts and Lobachev beamed. When the food and drink arrived all three men raised a toast to the tsar and then another to the continued improvement of trade and the triumph of Rus traders over their adversaries.

Then as they ate, Volkov finally inquired about Nizhni Novgorod. "You know, we have a visitor here in Moscow from those parts. The starets, Otyets Yakov, is with us." Lobachev nodded because his mouth was full of food. "He has become quite a popular figure."

Having swallowed his bit of bread, Lobachev agreed. "Just so was it in my town. We all vied to hear him preach. Ah, fine sermons did he give. They were not too hard to take. A healer too. I saw none of his healing myself, you understand, but I certainly heard of it."

"Yes, he's become an asset to our Moscow community," declared Volkov. "Unfortunately other things lately have created an unpleasant atmosphere in our city. We have had a series of murders of young women. Very disturbing. Frightening for the citizens as you can imagine."

"Yes, it must be so. You know, Sudar, I have heard of two similar crimes in my own town." Volkov leaned closer.

"Murders of two young women?"

"Yes."

"Ah, Master, it was three murders," piped up his man from the corner where he was sitting quietly feeding himself.

"Three, was it? Well, Volodika here, he hears more and sees more of what goes on in the streets than I do. He comes and goes for me on errands so it must be true."

"Was there an end to these vile deeds? Was the culprit apprehended?"

Lobachev turned to his man. "Answer the Magistrate's questions. You know more about the matter than I do."

"No one was caught, Sudar. But there have been no murders for months now. Gossip has it---." Volkov caught Lobachev shaking his head and so did Volodika who hesitated.

"No, no, go on with your story. I have an interest in hearing the rest of it," urged Volkov.

Lobachev's expression immediately changed to one of concern. "Yes, go on with your tale, the Magistrate is interested in hearing more," he ordered his man.

"Well," continued Volodika, "those in power who investigate such matters believe it was some stranger come to our town who has since left to commit his terrible crimes elsewhere. "

"Perhaps he left for Moscow," contributed Lobachev.

"Perhaps he did," said Volkov, agreeing with a nod. "Volodika, the last murder, when did it take place?"

"In October, Sudar. I remember because we have very little that is exciting happening in our Nizhni."

"Do you also recall the date of the first murder?"

"Ah, it came at the beginning of the summer. June it was. Yes, one murder was in late June, one in the heat of August, and the last in October, then thankfully no more."

"Interesting. Our murders are closer together. Three during Advent and one just last week. Tell me, Volodika, do you know how these women were murdered? The means used, that is?" Lobachev showed that the turn the conversation had taken was rapidly making him lose his taste for food.

"Why, Magistrate, they were all strangled I believe."

Lobachev groaned, "Oh, Volodika."

Volkov tried to reassure him. "Your man is being most helpful because just so were our young women slain." He saw the merchant's worried expression. "Surely you know I don't suspect either of you. I know you've only just arrived. But you can see that it is very likely that the murderer from Nizhni is now in our area. Indeed, if your man knows more," he added, turning to the servant, "and I hope that you do, why then, I wish to question him in greater detail." Lobachev pushed back his bowl.

"If you need him, you can have him. Anyway the

rascal likes to gossip and I usually can't spare the time to listen to him."

"This is rather more than gossip."

"Oh, I understand. But," said Lobachev, attempting a smile and failing, "it has rather taken away my appetite."

"Of course, of course. And I'm sure you're anxious to go about your business but leave your man with me a bit longer, eh?"

"He is at your service, Magistrate." Volkov rose; Lobachev rose. They exchanged felicitations and the merchant left.

Volkov sat down again and motioned Volodika to the bench his master had occupied.

"Now let's begin again. Here, have some more meat." He pushed a serving tray still full of food towards Volodika, whose appetite didn't appear in the least diminished by his recital of the murders. He ate and drank heartily as he talked.

"Our murderer left the victims near churches and shrines."

Volodika wrinkled up his brow thoughtfully, finally nodding, "Yes, I believe that was so in Nizhni as well. Though of the second one I don't really know as much. In August my master kept me busy running here and there. But you know, the gossip it collects, and I hear it all from my friends whenever I am back home again."

"This strangulation. Was it manual or were the victims garroted?"

"Manual, I believe. I recall someone mentioning it was done by someone's powerful hands."

"Were the victims also raped?" Volodika nodded since his mouth was full of food. Volkov leaned back and only after a long pause did he begin again. "Let me ask you still another question. When did Otyets Yakov first arrive in Nizhni?" Volodika was obviously no fool and he understand right away what was being asked. He didn't seem at all disturbed. Instead he gave Volkov a very shrewd glance.

"Yes, the fellow came to us in May and he left in late October."

"After the last murder?"

"Yes."

"Did you ever have occasion to meet this man?"

Volodika laughed. "Why I waited table for him when the chief merchants of the city hosted the fellow at a dinner. Yes, I myself put soup on the table before him and that disciple of his as well. Ah, Sudar, that disciple, he gave me shivers whenever he looked at me. That one can bring bad luck, I thought. Why, I felt as if a hare had crossed my path. I wouldn't try a staring contest with that one, I can tell you. No, I looked away and crossed myself. Now, Otyets Yakov, him I didn't mind so much; he was polite enough to me when I served him. I got to hear him preach too. Grateful, I was, for once not to hear about hell fire and demons and pincers tearing at one's flesh," concluded Volodika as he stuffed another bit of meat into his maw of a mouth and ground vigorously away at it. When he finished, he added, "Life is hard enough without hearing about unpleasantness in the next world too." Then he stabbed at still another piece of meat with his knife.

"Where," wondered Volkov, looking at the man's

spare frame, "does he put it all? Or does Lobachev forget to feed him?" Aloud he said, "Volodika, you may tell your master that you have been very useful to me." When the fellow was finally shown to the door, Volkov pressed coins into his hand.

"Thank you, thank you, Gosudar," repeated an overjoyed Volodika, bowing several times as he backed to the door. "May God's blessings be upon you."

After he'd left, Volkov sat down to make plans. "I shall have it out with the starets in spite of the Metropolitan." But he immediately had second thoughts. "This could make trouble for me at court. Should I risk it? Still, Antoniye is not in particular favor there. He is merely one more disposable prelate and the tsar has gone through so many already." The possible dismissal of the Metropolitan in disgrace brought a smile to Volkov's face. Then he thought about what he'd learned. "A lucky chance my learning this." It pleased him because it supported his suspicions but he felt some twinges of guilt as well because it also supported his bias against the starets. He reassured himself that it couldn't all be coincidence. "I must proceed against the man. A murderer has to be apprehended before the district is thrown into still more disorder. And truly no one looks as suspicious as Otyets Yakov. He would tie all the crimes together so neatly." He slapped his hand on the table. "Nor do I have time to send men to the ends of the earth asking questions about the fellow. I shall have to risk confronting him. And after all isn't it my duty to bring criminals to justice?" He felt suddenly vulnerable but shaking off his fears determined to go ahead in spite of them.

CHAPTER FOURTEEN

"Serezhenka, you've been pacing the floor the entire evening. What's amiss? What is causing all this restlessness?"
There was anxiety in Sofya's voice and Volkov hastened to reassure her. "It's nothing." She looked at him with disbelief. "Truly, it needn't concern you. It is a trifling matter only." "Trivial indeed! Why even Pavlushka was asking today what was wrong with Papa. And if a child notices, why then---? It's still those murders, is it not?" Volkov finally nodded, though with obvious reluctance. "Have you caught the fiend? I pray you have." When at last with a sigh he sat down in his chair at the head of the table, she put her hand tentatively on his arm, both to console and as a question.
"Yes, I'm convinced I've found the murderer. But to convince others and to bring him to justice that is

something else again. It will not be easy; it may actually be impossible. I am going to confront the man tomorrow."

"Surely it shouldn't be difficult. Why, you'll have your men with you and you can seize him without danger to yourself."

"It's more complicated than that. He must be made to admit his guilt." He paused then added, "And he has powerful friends."

"It isn't a boyar, is it, Serezhenka?"
"No, no, not this time," and they both recalled his last murder investigation and the high born murderer it had uncovered.

Sofya sat in silence, then suddenly looked up more appalled now than frightened. "Oh, surely not. I know you've disliked him since you met him but you cannot mean you suspect the starets. Tell me, please, that it's someone else." When he didn't reply, she felt her worst fears had been confirmed and shook her head vigorously. "For once your nose, as you call it, for these things must be leading you astray. Now if it were that hanger-on of his, then I could believe it. He is wicked; he hates women. I saw how he looked at us at Irina's, full of loathing and disgust. And what had we ever done to warrant such hatred? But the starets? Why, you yourself saw and heard him speak of holy things, of repentance, and of goodness. Can you deny the sincerity with which he spoke?"

Sofya, my dear," replied Volkov, dismissing her arguments about Fedka, who seemed of little consequence in his scheme of things, "you can't possibly know the evil of which even so-called good men are sometimes capable. They can so easily put on a false appearance that gulls the unwary."

"Then it is the starets that you insist on confronting tomorrow?"

"Yes, and not on some whimsical impulse, not just because of my nose for evil as you put it. I am not such a dolt." Sofya opened her mouth to reply but he continued his arguments. "There were similar murders in Nizhni Novgorod and they coincided with his residence there. They ceased abruptly when he left. He arrived in Moscow and they began here. So, am I just allowing my prejudices to place the guilt on him? No, decidedly not, and it is unjust of you to think so. It has to be him, don't you see that. And I've seen him with women. His avidity. Why, the man lusts after them; he indicated as much himself. And these young women were all forced."

Sofya put her hands to her face. "There is danger to you then for how will you ever get him to admit to such crimes?"

Volkov shrugged and then muttered. "There is just something about him---. Ah, surely if he believes at all in what he preaches and I don't think it is a complete pretense, he would want to rid his soul of these heinous sins by confessing. He would want to atone for the evil to which his lust has led him. So, I don't, you see, feel that he is a complete liar. In any case I shall find out tomorrow."

"And if he will not confess and complains to the authorities instead that you dishonor him then it is you that will be the one in trouble."

"Probably."

"Serezhenka, I wish you would not do this."

"I must." Seeing her saddened expression, Volkov wished he hadn't blurted out his worries. "It would have been better if I had not told you any of this."

"No, it's better to know the worst, then one can be prepared." She reached out to touch him again and he ended by pulling her onto his lap and burying his head between her breasts as she softly stroked his head.

Summoning his bailiff the following day, Volkov informed him of his plan for confronting the starets. The bailiff blanched, if, thought Volkov, a man with such a hairy face can show a loss of color. "Come, Mitka, you're acting like a devil that's just caught a paralyzing whiff of incense. The blame will fall on me if this fails; you'll probably be safe enough."

"Ah, ah," cried Mitka, throwing up his hands in a gesture of dismay, "probably be safe says my master but he is the one who insists on acting as if the sea is only knee deep. Sudar, you are defying the Metropolitan. Surely this is not a safe thing to do?"

"I put it to you that the starets is a charlatan and murderer and he must be exposed. The Metropolitan will cease supporting him once the starets is shown to be a villain."

"Master, the man's supporters here in the city will be furious at being made to look like fools. And their anger may not only fall on him."

"They will thank me for ridding the city of him. And I will not allow him to be merely passed on to still another community by confining myself to hopes that he will eventually go away and all this will stop."

"There is also Pugachev," said Mitka, continuing

his arguments in the wish that Volkov might reconsider. "He will be humiliated. He will know he has hung an innocent man."

"Pugachev knew my doubts but ignored them. I asked him to delay. Let it be shown that he acted rashly." He looked closely at his subordinate. "I see that at least now you agree the starets is the murderer."

"Of course, for have you not explained to me about the strangulations in Nizhni Novgorod. I agree that with so many cases it can't be mere coincidence. But how will you expose him? Surely he will deny everything."

"I will confront him with the facts. If he is stubborn, I will announce that I am going to the palace with these facts. I will say to him that there are those who will heed what I have to say. I will go over the head of the Metropolitan."

"And if he continues to deny his guilt?" asked Mitka, who looked stricken as soon as the palace was mentioned.

With a rueful expression, Volkov was forced to admit, "Then I shall really have to go to the palace."

"You mean you are going to try and trick him into a confession?"

"Of course. But if worse comes to worse, I will go to the palace. Surely I have some credit there." He thought for awhile. "Moreover neither our Prince nor his councilors have ever officially sanctioned this man. It is not Ivan who will be humiliated if the fellow is exposed. And when some of our citizens and an official or two are chagrined to learn they've feasted a villainous imposter it will not concern him unduly. He may even gain a bit of pleasure from seeing them look foolish."

"Still, it's a risky business, Sudar," groaned Mitka.

"Nonetheless, I intend to go on with my plan. This man has to be stopped. Justice has to be served." In a bitter voice he added, "It's been little enough observed in this realm."

Mitka offered one consoling note to himself as well as Volkov. "It's a good thing Otyets Jakov's friends, the Cossacks, have finally left for Sibir. Yes, yes, they left yesterday. At least we won't incur their wrath." He shrugged. "Ah well, if it must be, it must be," he concluded, sighing deeply.

"So we will go. And today. I have thought it through. Have two men ready to leave with us shortly."

"So small a troop? But, of course, we don't want to announce our intention to the Metropolitan. A small troop may look like an ordinary visit."

"Make sure Luka is one of the men accompanying us."

"Shouldn't he be left here?" To Volkov it looked as if even though Mitka was not eager to confront the starets, he also disliked allowing his chief rival for the Magistrate's attention to be in on the kill.

"Luka comes with us. I want my most trusted men." He accompanied Mitka out into the courtyard and waited while the bailiff issued orders for men and mounts. When the small troop was ready, it was still obvious from Mitka's expression that he was feeling less than martial. "You look as if you're going to your own execution," he told his bailiff. "Try to appear as if you have some confidence in what we're doing." But it was obvious that Mitka lacked just such faith in their mission.

Luka was sent ahead to make sure the starets was still in residence at the monastery to which Mitka had last tracked him and was not an honored guest at someone else's home. The men reached the gate and when Luka, waiting for them, nodded affirmatively, Volkov signaled him to summon the gatekeeper. The monk was startled by the sudden arrival of a small troop bristling with weapons and seemed paralyzed into inaction. Volkov had to soothe his fears by assuring him in mild tones that he had merely come to pay a call on the starets and asked politely if his men could be allowed to wait for him inside the monastic precincts. "We would be glad to show them hospitality, my Lord, while you visit our distinguished guest," stammered the gatekeeper once he'd recovered his voice. He then called for attendants to take everyone's horses. When Volkov walked away from his men, Mitka rushed after him.

"Are we to do nothing? Won't you need us?"

"Be patient. This is the way it has to be done. If a violent confrontation can be avoided, so much the better. But be alert. I may need you quickly and will send for you if I do." As his men were led away, Volkov noted that Mitka kept looking over his shoulder anxiously and was touched by his concern. Then he turned back to the gatekeeper who insisted on personally escorting the magistrate to the cell temporarily occupied by the starets. Rapping on the door, he announced Volkov's presence. Yakov himself responded to the knock. As he was shown into the room, Volkov noted with relief the absence of Fedka. After a hasty introduction the gatekeeper left, closing the door quietly behind him.

If the starets was surprised to see Volkov he gave no sign of it. He offered his guest the only bench in the austere little room and himself took a seat on the raised sleeping pallet near the small stove. Volkov took in the room. "Simple," he thought, "but not uncomfortable, even though a bit too warm. Obviously a place intended for guests." The heat made him pull off his hat and mittens. He tossed them on the floor near his seat and then opened his heavy coat as well.

"Settling in for a long visit?" asked the starets with a smile. "You're certainly welcome but if this visit is about the murder in your district, Magistrate, I've already told your man that I heard no cries for assistance that evening. Would that I had heard something. Why then the crime might have been prevented."

"What a smooth liar he is," reflected Volkov, quickly irritated by the man's poise and lack of concern. Aloud he announced, "I have a story to relate today and you will hear it through." A look of surprise appeared on Father Yakov's face at what amounted to a command. He leaned back, eyeing Volkov with a touch more wariness. "This tale, starets, begins far in the east, it reaches Nizhni Novgorod and will end here in Moscow."

The man smiled. "It sounds like the story of my travels."

"In a way it is just that. I have traced your steps, you see, from one place to another. Strange things happen in your vicinity. Things that concern me as an officer of the law."

"I can't imagine of what you are speaking?"

"I am speaking of rape and murder."

"Ah, yes, the investigation you are conducting. But what has that to do with me?"

Volkov felt his temper rising and had to fight to keep it under control. "Shortly after you arrived in Nizhni, a murder occurred, an exact duplicate of the ones here in Moscow" The starets was about to speak but Volkov stopped him. "Hear me out. There was another young woman slain there in August. Again, the pattern was the same, rape and strangulation. Still another murder was committed in late October. Then you came here and the murders ceased in Nizhni without a culprit being caught. It was believed by the authorities that the murderer had moved to other parts. And when you arrived in Moscow why then the murders began here, three in Advent and one---. Well, you've been questioned about that one. I say this is no mere coincidence but that it is you raping and murdering these young women." The starets put up his hands in a gesture of defense and began loudly protesting his innocence.

Volkov continued, raising his voice in order to be heard over Kozlov's objections, "Our first victim here in Moscow was a maidservant, the next a young girl returning from an errand of mercy to an old woman in her neighborhood. Your neighborhood as well that week. This was a young girl, surely you remember her. It was a snowy evening in this very district." And he named the date. "She was a fair little thing, dressed neatly in blue skirts and a red jacket. It was a virgin you forced. The third young woman---. This one happened in the Skorodom. Interestingly, you'd changed districts as well. The girl this time was a year or two older and perhaps a little bolder but not a wanton. Not someone who deserved rape and strangulation or to be left indecently exposed by the side of a church. And now we come to the latest victim, a young wife and mother, innocently bringing home a basket of mushrooms for her mother-in-law. She was dragged into a stable and like the others raped and strangled." In his anger, Volkov had risen and stood, fists clenched, growling his story into the face of the starets.

When the recital began, Father Yakov appeared dismayed and affronted but as Volkov continued a change came over his countenance. He began to shrink from Volkov's stare. "The basket of mushrooms. So it was that young woman who was murdered."

"So you admit that you met her, and further that you then forced and killed her."

"No, no I swear I didn't kill her. Indeed, she approached me. Yes, she came up to me as eagerly as they all do." He held out his hand in a pleading gesture. "As I said, it was she that approached me. Ostensibly asking for a blessing. You see, she'd heard I was in the neighborhood visiting the priest. She asked for a blessing but I knew what she really wanted. It's what they all want, these daughters of Eve. It is as I told you once, Magistrate, they are weak. They cannot control their desires. Why one could see that she wanted it just like all the others. Yes, yes, perhaps I remember them. But there was no rape. There is no question of rape here."

Volkov looked at the starets with disgust. "Liar. I saw the bruises on their arms, their torn clothing. Did you close your ears to their pleas? These girls were not willing; they were your victims." With his body Volkov began crowding the starets into a corner. The man was physically powerful but for the moment he seemed intimidated by the magistrate. "You fooled these poor young women into believing you a good man when in truth you are a devil."

"No, no, not that. It's untrue. I raped and murdered no one. Why, my man even compensated the women with coins for their time."

"If you believe that, you are lying even to yourself. Every one of these women you forced was strangled and dragged to some religious site, a wayside shrine, churches." The eyes of the starets widened with fear as Volkov leaned still closer. "What a vile hypocrite you are, preaching goodness and repentance and doing the opposite."

"I didn't murder them. And surely they were willing?" he pleaded.

"Damn you! Do you hear me? Damn you to hell, I say!" Yakov looked at Volkov, alarmed at his condemnation. "The devil may as well collect you now, for you are one of his. You will pay in this life and in the next," snarled Volkov. He put his hands on the shoulders of the starets, digging into the flesh with all his might.

The door was suddenly flung open. Fedka stood there taking in the scene. "What are you doing to my master?" he shrieked. "Take your hands from him. Do not touch him."

"Your master rapes and strangles young women and he will be punished for it." Volkov turned fully towards Fedka. "And what do you do for him, dispose of the bodies? Yes, it's you that drags the poor mutilated bodies away and displays them at holy places." In that minute, Volkov knew that what he'd said was true.

"Why? Why?"

"Fedka! Fedka!" cried the starets. "It was you, wasn't it? How could you? I told you to pay the women and send them away. It was you."

Before Volkov could take in all that was being shouted by the starets, he found himself under attack by Fedka who was still shrieking, "You will not touch my master." Suddenly Volkov found himself overborne and hurled to the floor with Fedka's strong hands around his own throat. The man's mad, he thought, as he struggled to break Fedka's grip. He kicked and tore at the man's arms with no success and was about to lose consciousness when suddenly Fedka's hold was broken and he was hurled into a corner of the room by the starets. As Volkov struggled to rise, he saw that the noisy struggle had brought a number of monks to the open door curious to know what was happening. Over their protests, the starets shut the door in their faces then assisted Volkov to the bed.

Volkov felt his throat. It was some time before he was able to speak and then it was only a hoarse croak. Meanwhile Fedka had begun weeping loudly in the corner and was ceaselessly wringing his hands. Volkov tried to speak again and at last he was able to whisper, "Let's hear the whole truth for once."

"Fedka, how could you do this?" asked the starets.

"Master," cried his man, "These creatures caused you to sin. They led you astray. They tempted you. I had to destroy them. Surely what is wicked must be destroyed. Do you see, Master, I placed them near those holy places as sin offerings."

"Ah, Fedka," groaned the starets. He covered his face with his hands and sank to the floor himself.

Volkov drew close, disgusted at his inability to make a decent sound, he again resorted to a whisper. "It was you," he hissed. "You began it all. You're as guilty as he is." He stopped and swallowed painfully. Speaking was just too difficult but he made an effort, went to the door and opened it. Then still in a whisper he told one of the monks waiting outside, "Get my men."

When they came and Mitka saw Volkov sitting on the bed carefully touching his bruised throat, he cried out, "Sudar, what has happened to you?" He looked around the room at the starets sitting with his head in his hands and at Fedka weeping copious tears in the corner.

"Have they confessed?" he asked Volkov and the magistrate nodded. He turned to Luka and the others, "Take them away." The monks began to protest but Mitka shouted them down.

"It is as my Lord here has said, these are wicked, wicked men in whom you have foolishly placed your trust and they are coming away with us now." Luka thrust back the monks and hauling Fedka up from the floor began to bind him.

"And this one too?" he asked.

"No, no, I will go peacefully," said the starets. Suddenly he began to beat his head with his hands and to howl like an animal in pain, startling everyone.

Volkov stared at Yakov with continued disgust but he was also surprised at the man's collapse. He'd expected more lying and protesting and resistance. After all he could have placed all the blame on Fedka. "Fedka the murderer!" he thought. That was a revelation. Yet it all made sense. The devoted servant protecting his master. The man returning late after murdering the witnesses to Yakov's transgressions. And in fact blaming those poor women for his master's sins. He leaned over to Mitka and said softly, "You'll come with me to the abbot. Luka and the others can take the prisoners to our lockup. But let me rest a minute first." Mitka nodded, his countenance still expressing concern. Volkov shook his head. "I shall be all right," he assured him.

CHAPTER FIFTEEN

Volkov was sitting in his armchair at the head of the table, His head was tilted back and a frowning Sofya was changing the poultice on his throat. "It feels good whatever it is," he murmured.

"It's dried spongilla grass mixed with water." She straightened up and looked at him with a serious expression. "Ah, Serezhenka, that man could have killed you."

Volkov made a deprecatory gesture, dismissing the danger he'd faced. "Well, he didn't."

"But your throat. It still has the marks on it and it's been several days now."

"You were right about Fedka. Of course I was right about the starets."

"Never mind them. I don't care about them. I worry about you and you've been out and about in spite of your condition when you should have been allowing yourself to recover."

"It can't be helped and today Ivan Andreyevich has summoned me to appear. I have to go."

"Could he be angry, do you think, for being made to look a fool. I mean, because he invited the starets to his home?" Volkov shrugged. "Irina's husband was furious. It is most unfair; he encouraged her in the first place."

"Encouraged Irina? I rather doubt she needed encouraging."

"Well, he agreed readily enough when she asked if she could introduce the starets to her friends. So he shouldn't blame her now."

Sofya frowned at the injustice. "The Boyarina Trubetskoya complained to her husband that she had been taken in by a charlatan. Her husband in turn took Irina's man to task and so he scolded her. Yet that woman begged Irina for an invitation. I do hope Ivan Andreyevich doesn't give you a difficult time. And you haven't heard from the Metropolitan. Oh, what a lot of difficulties you've incurred." She leaned over and kissed him. "Still, these were terrible crimes and I'm glad justice will be done."

"Never mind about my troubles, it will all come right." I hope, he added silently. "I shall want my boots and coat. Mitka is coming for me and we'll ride together to the Shuisky residence. I'll see what happens. And at least it's a clear, sunny day."

"And biting cold."

"I can bundle up against that." Before he could get out the door he found himself wrapped up against the cold like a child. Sofya insisted on wrapping a voluminous scarf around his neck over his protests that he wasn't Pavlushka. Then to please her because he knew she was still worried about him, he ceased his complaints

An hour later after some small delays, he and Mitka arrived at the Shuisky residence. Ivan Andreyevich came out onto the porch to greet his guest. He shouted to his steward to take good care of Mitka and then personally escorted Volkov into the hall. "Enter, enter, the threshold, particularly on a cold day, is no place for prolonged greetings." At least, thought Volkov, his smile seems to indicate he bears me no grudge.

"Sit," ordered Shuisky and he bellowed for refreshments. "Bread and salt, and yes, vodka, a good draught will do wonders for that throat of yours." Volkov looked at him in surprise. "Of course I know about that. I already have most of the details. I know how you single-handedly fought off those two villains. And you thought I might be angry? I was, I was. But not with you, my dear fellow. No, it was with that rogue who had fooled us all.

"It was the church, Volkov. All those haughty prelates are ultimately responsible. They think to lead us about by the nose. Why they lauded the fellow to the heavens. But you exposed him for the villain he is." Shuisky leaned closer. "I was there when Ivan interviewed the Metropolitan about the affair. I've never liked that weasel Antoniye. It was a pleasure witnessing the fellow's humiliation. Why, the fellow turned as white as snow and shook in those fancy slippers of his. And the tsar roared, 'Is the church sanctifying rapists now?' The

Metropolitan of course immediately laid the blame on the bishop of Nizhni Novgorod who will no doubt blame the bishop of Perm who will blame the abbot of some still more distant monastery." He suddenly sat back with a puzzled expression on his face. "Volkov, how could this happen? How could so many folk, and not credulous peasants either, be taken in by this man? Can you understand it?"

"I've been thinking of nothing else, Ivan Andreyevich," replied Volkov. "My feelings underwent change whenever I met the man though I felt antipathy towards him from the very beginning of our acquaintance."

Shuisky nodded. "Yes, after the villain was exposed my chaplain came to me. He informed me that he'd had his own suspicions from the beginning. So I asked, well, why didn't you tell me. He said he'd voiced those same doubts to you."

"That's true. And the man was a good preacher. I was impressed with what he said and on other occasions he disarmed me both with his words and with his deeds and yet there was always something about the man that troubled me, that made me uneasy."

"Ah, yes, your instincts told you he was a bad fellow. Sound instincts those."

"Ivan Andreyevich," continued Volkov, "it was as if he were two men. Really two men. He was not pretending, I think. He was a man with a mission and wished to do good and to be good but he had an evil side that gave in to the devil's temptations. He lied to himself. He didn't want to believe himself capable of such sins. Ah, it is all very difficult to explain."

"He'll pay for his crime. Here, drink some more. You've probably strained your voice telling me all of this. Anyway I had to let you know the Tsar is even more impressed with your skills in detection than before. Nikita Romanov put in a good word as well and so did Boris Godunov. For once those two agreed on something and it was on your talents and persistence. I even gained a bit of praise for sponsoring you for your present office. Yes, it all came out that the Metropolitan had forbidden your investigation. So it seems you've acquired a bit more fame."

Volkov appeared more rueful than happy about this. Shuisky grinned at him, understanding perfectly. "Take it with good grace, kinsman. You are not so prominent yet that it can make life difficult. It can only do you good." I hope so, thought Volkov, though he would have preferred his previous anonymity.

Shuisky sat back and smiled at Volkov. "My two sons should be here shortly. You must tell us the whole story. Indeed, my dear Volkov, you should be able to dine out on this story for some months to come." Volkov let out a groan and Shuisky laughed and laughed.

The interview with the Metropolitan was easier than Volkov thought it would be. Antoniye was quite subdued. The only glares he received were from the clerics in the reception chamber, but he noted that he was not kept waiting this time. He bowed to the prelate; Antoniye asked him to be seated and immediately ordered refreshments served. At first the prelate said nothing much. He merely kept running his hands up and down the arms of his throne. When he finally did speak he had to clear his throat several times.

"Magistrate, it seems we were in error. The starets deceived us all." In a pleading voice he asked, "But after all what were we to think since he was so highly recommended by other churchmen? His demeanor was so---. But now we've learned the truth he shall be punished. This Fedka has taken no orders and in no way falls under the jurisdiction of the church. You may have him. Hang the fellow as soon as possible." Antoniye shuddered sanctimoniously. "May God have mercy on his soul. As to Otyets Yakov. Ah, we still find this difficult to believe. Why his sermons, the incidents of healing---? How wily the devil is, sending such a man to us." He sighed as if in acute pain which Volkov thought highly likely. A pain of spirit as well as of body what with the scolding he'd received from Ivan.

"We could turn the starets over to you but an alternative has been suggested by our Prince himself. As you know there is a monastery of some renown located on the White Sea coast. Or perhaps you didn't know. The place is famed for its austerity. And the Tsar---," Antoniye was at this point forced to pause and clear his throat and visibly winced. Perhaps, thought Volkov with satisfaction, he's recalling a particular moment of his interview with Ivan. "Well, the Tsar, as I was saying, suggested that since the starets has such hot blood it might be cooled by permanent residence among the ice and snow of the north. So we propose to exile him there. If he attempts to leave, he forfeits his life. Our Prince thought this a fitting punishment. We do too. Does it meet with your approval?"

Volkov nodded. "Yes," he replied. To himself he

murmured, of course I'll agree since it was Ivan that suggested it. If Antoniye won't naysay the Tsar, does he think I will do so? And perhaps it is a fitting punishment. A few further comments by the Metropolitan and Volkov was dismissed. At first he felt a sense of vindication then just as suddenly a mood of depression returned. It had been an altogether dirty business, he told himself. With a sigh he went to seek out Mitka and they left the Kremlin precincts together. In the square outside, Volkov pointed towards a kabak and they broke their fast in that establishment.

"So it's all over, eh, Mitka?"

"Yes, Sudar, except for the hanging. But what exactly is to become of the starets?" Volkov told him the tsar's solution.

"That is a good notion. Our Prince is as wise as Solomon." He glanced at Volkov and saw that he was frowning. "Do you disagree? Would you rather have had him hung?"

"No, probably not." Volkov tried to shake off his momentary malaise. "Mitka, let the families know when Fedka is to be hung. Sveta's people too, and Semyon's master. For Fedka confessed to that crime as well. To Pugachev's dismay." Mitka nodded. "At least they can see the fellow pay for his crimes." Volkov sank back into a contemplative mood and didn't say anything for awhile which suited Mitka as he busy with his meal.

"You know," he began again, "it is strange how the devil bound those two together with the same rope."

"It's over now though, Sudar, and what a relief, I say. As for Fedka, well, he'll receive the sovereign remedy against all ills." Volkov looked a question at his bailiff. "Death, Sudar, death. And I can't say I'm sorry. He was a wicked fellow. I for one never liked the fellow." He ended this pronouncement with another big bit of his bread. Volkov stared at him then suddenly laughed.

"At least it's over and we can concentrate on other things, on trivialities and enjoy the festivities again."

"But, Sudar, Lent isn't far away. Another season of fast."

Volkov groaned. "I've lost all track of time." But he smiled at his bailiff. "Then we shall have to make the most of what's left of this season."

Glossary

Bannik-Spirit of the bathhouse. Wealthier Muscovites had saunas on their properties and believed firmly in the efficacy of the steam bath.

Bliny, blinis-Russian equivalent of the crepe.

Boyar-nobleman; boyarina-noblewoman

Domovoy-house spirit. Mollified by offerings of food and drink, the domovoy brought good luck to his particular household.

Kabak-tavern

Kutya-Traditional Christmas fare, a dish made up of grain, honey, and poppy seeds.

Hetman-Cossack chieftain, sometimes written as ataman.

Leshy-shape changing forest spirit

Metropolitan-highest member of the Russian Orthodox clergy; he deferred to the Patriarch of the

church whose residence was in Istanbul, once
Constantinople.

Moroz-the frost demon
Muzhik-a Russian peasant

Ostrog- frontier fort, similar to the wooden block
forts of the American frontier but here the frontier
was in the east at the Ural Mountains which the
Russians were just beginning to penetrate.

Otyets-father

Roubles, kopecks, dengi-denominations of coins,
listed in descending order.

Rusalki-maidens who were usually guardians of
life-giving waters. They could lure men to their
deaths in pools and ponds.

Sarafan-basic woman's garment, a floor length

jumper.

Skazhi-tales, stories

Starets-wandering preacher, sometimes a healer as well.

Strelets (singular), streltsy (plural)-Musketeers, created by Ivan IV as guards, even sometimes acting as firefighters in the city of Moscow.

Sudar-lord, master; Gosudar-used for those of even higher rank.

Tsar-emperor, title used by Ivan IV who also retained the older title of Grand Prince of Muscovy.

Yermak Timofeyevich-first Rus (Russian) conqueror of Siberian land.

Yurodivyi-holy fool, much revered in old Russia.

Made in the USA
Middletown, DE
02 April 2020